MASTER OF THE MEET CUTE

MASTER OF THE MEET CUTE

CASSIE MAE

Dedicated to Jon Jon, for being a movie buff…
Never mind. You'll never read this book.

Dedicated to Jenny,
The sibling who reads ALL my books. You're the best :D

Landon's Watch Party!

Landon is a film buff, and there are many references and parallels in his top ten movies and what goes on in his life. If you want to watch along, here is the full list and the themes that inspired them to be included.

Landon's Top Ten Movies (as of April, 2012. We all know it's going to change.)

#10: *ALADDIN*

1992

DIRECTED BY: JOHN MUSKER AND RON CLEMENTS

My very first movie needs to be on the list. I was four, but I remember it clear as day. The smell of the room—bacon. The color of the carpet—green. The singular sunbeam that stretched across the floor, hitting my sneakers—blue and orange, with the light up heels.

I clutched a fuzzy wolf-print blanket in one arm, a cup of bright red juice in the other. Yep, it was red. Kool-Aid. Cherry.

And when the genie burst from the lamp, my cup tilted, dripping like a leaky faucet onto the carpet.

I sat slack-jawed the entire movie from that point forward. Genie was (and remains) my all-time favorite character. I waited the entire movie to see Aladdin free him.

Freedom... what a foreign word for a four-year-old. But it stuck. Why? Not sure. Could be the fact that when Dad spotted the cup in my hand, dripping generously onto the carpet for a good thirty minutes, he let out a sound I can only describe as a dinosaur getting crushed by a meteor. Not that I know what that sounds like, but I can imagine Dad got pretty damn close.

And I wanted to burst free from the living room right then and there.

He ripped the cup from my hand, rushing into the kitchen where Mom was. His booming, dinosaur voice said choice words I don't remember. Oh, but I remember the feeling.

Mom yelled back. Dad came in with an entire roll of paper towels, shoving me to the side while he stamped on the red puddle. More words spilled from his lips, all directed at Mom.

Why red Kool-Aid? Why an open cup? Why on his brand new carpet?

Master of the Meet Cute

I grappled for the remote, determined to drown out his voice. I knew the buttons—I was well-versed in them by then, being an avid Saturday morning cartoon watcher. Ironically, it was Dad who taught me how to use the remote. He settled me onto his lap in his favorite recliner, explaining every button and what it meant. He made me promise never to pass the one-five on the volume.

But I couldn't hear. And Jafar was in a lamp, Genie flicking him into the sky. The moment for Genie's freedom had to be close... if it was going to happen at all.

The volume ticked to something in the threes, increasing more than I've ever done before. My heart pounded; I was up on my knees, eyes large and dry, refusing to blink so I wouldn't miss it.

And the remote disappeared.

No... It was ripped from me, almost like he'd ripped my arm off.

His hand was hot—almost like that one time I'd touched the front burner. It shocked me from the TV, and I looked Dad straight in the eye. His face was the color of my Kool-Aid, maybe darker. His jaw was locked tight, something pulsing in his temples.

It's important to mention that Dad never hit me. He's also not a horrible person. But that volume must've been the last straw that day for him. I've never moved so fast in my life, bolting down the hall to my room.

The sound of the movie faded, muffled by the pillow I used to hide my head.

It would be another two years until I found out if Aladdin held up his end of the deal.

But when I did, when I finally watched the end—at Alec's house, sitting with an empty bowl of popcorn and water, because I refused any colored drink after that day—I understood why people love not just this movie, but all movies.

There is adventure, life, hope.

And happily ever afters.

ONE

"I'm sorry, sir, but the warranty states—"

"I don't give a shit what the warranty says." The faceless man on the other end of the line huffs. My muscles are so clenched my ass could crack a walnut. "Get me your supervisor."

I manage to keep my own exasperated sigh under control, swallowing it into the hollow pit of my gut. *Last call for the day, Landon. Then you can high-tail it out of here.*

My customer service voice is slowly disappearing, morphing into the robotic recitation of the warranty for car batteries. With a farewell from my disgruntled friend I'd like to repeat—but I'd get fired in a heartbeat—the line clicks, and my shoulders relax.

Call centers are the worst. They pay well and give me benefits and work around my school schedule…

And suck the life out of me every time I pick up the phone.

I turn my phone off as quickly as I can, typing up the incident report and saving it in the ancient computer system. Rumor has it they're switching over within the next month, which means a lot of training is coming my way.

Yay.

My phone buzzes in my pocket, and I flick my gaze to the clock in the right corner of my computer. Ten-o-three. Shit. I'm going to be late.

First class of my very last semester, and I'm going to make one hell of an impression by walking in twenty minutes after the assignment is given.

I groan and crack as I stand. I really got to cut this hunched-over shit out. I'm only twenty-three for Christ's sake.

I swipe my laptop and stick my trusty Beetlejuice baseball cap on my head to cover the headset hair. Then I clock out and rush to the street to grab a cab. I'd say that living in New York means I save a lot in gas—because I never drive my car—but boy do I make up for it in cab fare and Subway fees.

My feet crunch against the snow and salt along the walkway into the school. I'm not *terribly* late, but late enough that I might not get a seat. It's not like there will be much else for me to learn, though, to be honest. This last course is a must for my major, but the Future Filmmakers grant is the reward for the final project prize, and I'm using it to make my satirical zombie flick. I have to hit the market now, since it's getting big—zombies and all.

The Walking Dead debuted three years ago, and it shot to the number one TV series. I was writing this zombie parody way before then—since my junior year… of *high school.* If I time it right, I can capitalize on a huge and hungry audience.

My brain is all marketing and money when I walk into the loud classroom. Theater types don't tend to be quiet. I spot Jace, a good buddy of mine, across the stage and make my way to him. We've been in the same classes since freshman year. He's majoring in the acting stuff though, while I want behind the scenes. If I get the grant, I'm casting him in a second.

Since the class is held in one of the many auditoriums at NYU, we're on the stage, footsteps echoing as each person shuffles for a seat. The chairs are kinda all over the place, set up in groups of four or five. I find an empty one and tuck my hand around the top.

As soon as I lift it off its legs, a thump rumbles my feet, and a high-pitched squeak pierces my ears. Something smacks my foot, pushing the melted snow through the breathable holes and into my sock. I jolt, my gaze shooting to the source.

I'm suddenly three years old. It's 1992. I'm in my living room, drinking Kool-Aid. And Aladdin has just spotted Jasmine, and he's instantly hypnotized.

I picture that dumb look on his face. That look I've never possessed in my life. The look I thought was only in movies, only made for movies. That look is not real. That feeling that entices that look is not real.

Love at first sight is not a thing. Infatuation? Sure. But love? Well, I don't think love happens at all—at least not the kind in movies.

But if there was such a thing… if for one second the universe decided to throw me a bone and say, "Hey, Landon, sometimes stuff in the movies happens in real life. I'll prove it." It would be this second. This one second that lasts a lifetime. My eyes lock onto the most beautiful girl I've seen in my life.

And I just knocked her flat on her ass.

The chair in my hand suddenly weighs a thousand pounds.

"I-I-I am so sorry," I stutter. Her bright green eyes drift up my ragged jeans, my Back to the Future t-shirt, to my Beetlejuice cap. I let the chair go with a crash that echoes in my ears, and I reach for her. "I didn't know… I thought that chair was free."

She takes my hand. Her nail polish is pink. Chipped. Only remnants. Like she picks at it when she's bored or thinking.

Don't know why the hell I'm so focused on that nail polish. Don't know why I find it so damn adorable.

She fixes her long blonde ponytail, swinging it over her shoulder. "It's okay."

Dear God, help me. She has a southern accent.

"Uh…" My voice is a stranger. Swear to God, I've never croaked as much as I have in the dozen words I've just uttered. I rub the back of my head, my fingers catching on my baseball cap. "Here. It's all yours." I fix the chair, hoping I come off like a gentleman. Ignore the red I'm sure is splashed all up and down my face. I'm one of those cool guys who blushes a lot.

"Thanks." She gives me a smile. There's a gap between her front two teeth. Not a wide gap, not a small gap. The perfect gap.

I blink. Stare too long. Picture Jim Carrey in The Mask when he turns into a wolf and his tongue lolls across the table.

Her hand wraps around the chair, her chipped nails snagging my attention again, and she drags it toward another group. My eyes follow the sway of her hips.

I need to date more. I'm well out of practice.

I shake my head and stalk over to Jace chair-free, and he's laughing his ass off.

"Smooth."

My lips turn up in amusement, but it's far from what I feel. I'm still gob smacked by what just happened. "That's what I was going for." I take a spot on the floor, crossing my ankles. Jace plops down next to me. A few more late-comers filter in, and since there are no more chairs, they take up a spot of stage a couple feet away from us. At least I'm not the latest person here.

The professor walks in a few minutes later, and I adjust to a more comfortable position. The class is still buzzing, and the professor doesn't look like he cares all that much over the noise. He's probably used to a loud crowd given his theater background.

"All right, everyone…" He rolls the sleeves on his pink

striped button down. It sits under a sweater vest that looks straight out of Chandler Bing's closet. "I'm Professor Driver, and I'm aware most of you are in here for that grant money, so let's just get into it."

Someone lets out a laugh-hiccup combo, and I smirk, my gaze drifting toward the stunning girl I dropped to the floor. Her eyes were already on me, but they dart away so quickly I'm not sure if I imagined it.

Professor Driver shakes a bean can, a jumble of dice-sounding blocks crashing around the inside. "This project is to write, direct, and act in a short film." He heads to the group to his right, the one with the gorgeous girl, and holds out the can. "Your genre will be random. Work in groups of four or five, and come up with a crew."

"Do not put me in as writer," Jace mutters next to me, and I stifle a laugh. Jace has dyslexia, but he goes above and beyond when it comes to memorizing lines, and everyone who's been in these classes with him knows it. He has lead actor in the bag.

"Don't have to tell you this is a hundred percent of your grade," Professor Driver says as he starts around the room. "All films will be shown at the festival at the end of the semester, and the group that receives the most votes gets the grant. Good luck."

The class quickly groups up, and I'm ready to rush over to the girl with those green eyes, but the latecomers wander over and take a spot next to Jace and I, and it looks like she's already paired with the others sitting in her circle.

Damn.

The professor stops in front of her, and she dips her hand into the can, pulling out a smooth-looking black rock with some words scribbled on the underside.

Professor Driver walks around the stage, answering questions. The other two in our group introduce themselves—Audrey and Josh, brother and sister. Jace gets his lady-killer smile in place, and I prepare for a long semester of him and this girl hooking up. It wouldn't be the first time for him, and certainly not the last.

My gaze lands on this girl I can't seem to look away from for more than a minute, and she's looking at me…

Then she's not.

Maybe I could score some pointers from my good buddy. Even though that's embarrassing as hell. And I've never been one to nail and bail, so his advice probably wouldn't hold much weight, anyway.

I don't know how to execute the love stuff. I'm better at the gore, the drama, the action. That's my forte. That's my passion. My zombie script prods in the back of my mind, and I rip my gaze from the gorgeous green-eyed girl.

Love is for the movies.

The professor makes his way to my group sitting on the floor, and I stick my hand in, feeling only one rock left in the mix.

"So many choices," I joke as I pull it out. That's what we all get for walking in late, I'm guessing. I turn the rock over in my hand. Please give me horror. If not horror, mystery. If not mystery, superhero or action. Just anything but—

"Romantic comedy," Jace reads over my shoulder.

Well… shit.

Two

"You want to do the script?" Jace asks Audrey. He's being uncharacteristically productive, and it's all to get into her pants. If there wasn't a grant on the line, I'd probably play wingman.

"I got it," I say, typing my name into the spreadsheet on my laptop. I've already have me in as director. Josh volunteered for cameraman, and I pray to God he not only knows how to operate one but follows my lead on how I want it shot.

Audrey's lips twitch in the corner. "I don't mind doing the script."

"Might be easier if we work on it together," I offer, even though an anxious niggle runs up my arm as I type her name next to mine. Group projects are the bane of my educational existence. I learned my lesson early in high school. I got into advanced film studies—obviously my top pick for the electives—and our first assignment was a documentary-style film. Since I was the freshman, I let everyone else assign roles while I studied how a crew works. Turns out, the crew *didn't* work. After three weeks, with only two days left and no footage, I grabbed a camera and shot it myself. Pulled off a B… for the group.

I rub my hand over the back of my Beetlejuice cap, tipping it to see my screen better. Yeah… with money on the line, I'm going to have my hands in every single aspect of this film.

Jace leans into Audrey. "He's real easy-going, don't you think?"

She giggles, and I resist the urge to kick him in the shin.

Jace doesn't let up on the flirting. He's a natural at it—the charisma, the charm… It's why he'll be great leading actor material for this romantic comedy, so a bonus point there, I guess. Don't know how the hell he does it.

My focus drifts upward, peering over the top of my laptop to the girl that stun-locked me not ten minutes ago. She's crisscross applesauce in that chair I tried to take, tracing her finger over the seam in her jeans. For the life of me, I can't pinpoint a perfect comparison. This girl has the hair of Jennifer Lawrence, the tooth gap of Felicity Jones, Emma Stone's smile, Drew Barrymore's cheeks… It's like I've seen her a million times before today, filling different screens through my whole life.

Yet… she's completely new—a mole on her chin, right under her bottom lip. The hollow of her neck deepens when she inhales. One of the sleeves on her fuzzy sweater is flipped up at the edge, something a wardrobe specialist would fix before the director calls action.

A blurry hand interrupts my view, a loud snap cracking

through my ears.

I blink into focus. "Huh?"

Jace chuckles, dropping his hand. "You sure you want to take on all this shit?"

I clear my throat, forcing my gaze to the open laptop resting on my thighs. "I prefer it."

"So do we," Audrey jokes, and Josh and Jace agree with vehement nods. Looks like Audrey and Josh don't have a problem with my steamrolling.

The only problem I see is the damn genre I pulled. If only all of us came with the natural talent to woo women.

I tab to the browser and start searching popular romantic comedies within the last decade. Jace snorts as I add Miss Congeniality, Bridesmaids, and Sweet Home Alabama to my watch list. I've got to study. I'm not letting this derail my train to directorial success.

"Make sure to include a great kissing scene," Jace says, kicking his legs out in front of him and giving Audrey a wink. She rolls her eyes and smacks his shoulder. Josh pulls his phone out and becomes invested in whatever is on the screen while his sister and Jace flirt more.

I type into my search bar: *beats of romance*. There are beats to horror, so I assumed correctly that romance would have them, too. Luckily, I'm versed in comedy already, but rom com is a completely different animal. And that stupid sense of overwhelm starts creeping in, tightening my shoulders.

I look up again, my gaze bee-lining straight to the girl.

It stays until she catches me, then I pretend to read the article on my computer.

It happens at least four more times in the next two minutes.

"I can ask her out for you," Jace says, lifting a brow.

"Huh?"

"Don't act stupid." He nods toward the girl. "You can't stop looking at her."

"I'm *thinking*." It's not complete bullshit. I am definitely thinking. Thinking about that sprinkle of laughter, that southern accent, that gap between her teeth, where she's from, what she likes to do, what part she's taking in her group—if she's a director like me or would rather act...

"Just get off your ass and ask her." Jace kicks me in the shin, and the sting runs up my leg and into my numb butt. Next time I'll get here early enough for a chair.

I ignore his attempts at getting me to put myself out there. Work first, flirt second. It's my motto. And work is never done.

Besides, love is one of those things that looks vastly different on film than it does in reality. My parents barely talk to each other, and when they do, it's sarcastic bites and back-handed compliments. I've seen them kiss once. When I was seven. Ma lost her wedding ring down the drain, and Dad fished it out. It was the most affection I'd witnessed until I got to high school. Then I witnessed all sorts of affection in the hallways, and that was... not as great as the movies.

I blow out a sigh and start reading reviews for Bridesmaids. Critics and audiences praised Kristen Wiig's performance, and Melissa McCarthy for the comedic sidekick. Melissa's been nominated for nearly every award this year—it'll be interesting to see if she wins.

Looks like it's more of a raunchy comedy, but the chemistry between Kristen and Chris O'Dowd has been highly praised in all the fan forums.

All right…

I hit the search bar and type: *How to create chemistry.*

The first thing to pop up is 13 QUICK AND EASY TIPS TO CREATE CHEMISTRY WITH A GIRL.

Damn it, I look right at her again. This girl is the only one in existence to take my attention from work. She nods at the person across from her, a strand of blonde hair falling from her ponytail. Her fingernail drags over her bottom lip.

She catches me staring. Smiles. Red splashes her cheeks. She offers a wave.

"You looking up pointers?" Jace asks with a snort. "How long has it been?"

"It's research," I half-lie as I click into the article. I absolutely need the tips for directing this project from hell. But I won't admit I'm curious about the tips for personal reasons that have everything to do with the girl across the room.

Number one: use her name or give her a unique nickname to use in conversation.

Well, shit. I don't know her name.

Number two: make eye contact.

At least I'm winning there.

Number three: make her laugh.

It goes on and on about teasing and being playful and shit. I pull out my notebook and make a list. Elle, my sister, used to make fun of me for always writing stuff down when I'm on my laptop. "Just use Word or notepad." But I prefer the real thing. Something about putting pen to paper makes it stick.

I go through all thirteen tips and tricks. I'm a bit skeptical about some—mirroring movements feels weird, but I'll give it a shot. My notebook is a scribbled mess by the time class gets dismissed.

"Should we meet this weekend?" Josh asks as I stuff my notes and laptop into my bag.

"Sure. I'll make a schedule and share it with you guys."

"I can do it if you wa—"

"I got it," I rush out, throwing the strap of my bag over my shoulder. Pins and needles poke my sleepy feet as I chase after the girl I'm ready to practice all this chemistry stuff on.

I've got my opener. I spent the last twenty minutes practicing it in my head. She's halfway through the quad when I catch up with her. My heart's a pounding mess, and I chalk it up to the fact that I had to jog and not because I'm nervous as hell.

Tip number seven: use respectful and non-sexual touches. I reach for her elbow, tapping lightly for her attention.

"Would you like an opportunity to embarrass me?" I say, falling into step with her. "So we're even."

Thank you, Christ, for the time to practice that line. Not a tremble in my voice, and I even got a half smile thing going on that I guess is a slam dunk in these romance movies. It was mentioned no less than fifteen times in the articles I looked up.

She meets my gaze, those green eyes sort of hypnotizing… but not nearly as much as the burst of laughter that spills from her lips.

"You worked on that line for the last hour and half, didn't you?"

Holy hell, she's a genius. "Did it work?"

A red flush falls over her cheeks, and she focuses on the sidewalk. "Maybe."

Okay… I've got the signs. The blush, the teasing, the laughter, the suppressed grins… Whoever wrote that article knows what they're talking about. It's probably a woman. I'll send her a million thank you cards if this pans out.

I take two larger steps, trusting myself not to fall on my ass so I can face her while she continues walking. "I'm a terrible singer. We could go to a karaoke bar."

That's not a lie. I have musical theater this semester as well, and it's not going to be pretty.

"Hmmm…" She puts a finger to her chin. "No good. I'm eighteen and no fake ID."

Freshman. Yep… a genius. The class we have is usually reserved for upperclassmen. She just became ten thousand percent sexier.

"All right. Something else then." I'm not giving up. Another awesome tip was to not assume every no was a rejection when it came to inviting her to do activities.

She stops walking, and my feet stop, too. I keep the eye contact thing going, but it's really not that hard. She has gorgeous eyes.

"How about bowling?" she suggests.

"Ah… See, that wouldn't work. The point is to embarrass *me*." Wow, this cockiness is coming out pretty naturally, especially since I'm well out of practice. "Not embarrass you twice, Tumbles."

I'd like to say the nickname was planned, but it tumbled off my lips. How fitting.

She lifts a brow. "Think you're that good, huh?"

"I know I am." Again, not lying. It's one of the few sports I am good at. Alec and I often found ourselves at the bowling alley when I couldn't stand the constant bickering at home.

Her hip juts. "Then embarrassing you will be more fun than I thought."

I am not a romantic… if researching how to have this conversation was any indication. But I swear I hear a hallelujah chorus. My hand goes to the back of my cap, and I'm grinning like a damn fool when I blurt, "You free tomorrow night?"

And magic words pop out from her, right through that adorable gap. "I'm free right now."

#9: THE BIG LEBOWSKI

1998

DIRECTED BY JOEL COEN

I saw my first on-screen boob at nine years old, and it was in front of my dad.

Alec and I were hanging out at his house, like usual. My house wasn't for friends—Dad often got annoyed when someone was there when he got off work, and Mom always told us to go outside when we stepped foot into the house. Since it was around thirty degrees that day, we were in Alec's basement, blankets tucked around us, courtesy of his mom, and N64 controllers in our hands.

Heavy footsteps carried down the stairs, and Alec and I gave each other this look like a monster was coming. Alec's mom was tiny—barely five feet. Both of us were about as tall and thick as she was.

My dad, however, is a beast of a man. Large belly, size fifteen shoes, six-four. His frame filled the basement doorway, and my stomach dropped into my shoes.

What did I do? I ran through all my shenanigans, but considering I wasn't a particularly rebellious kid, and Alec certainly wasn't either, I came up empty.

"Hey, Dad." My race car crashed into a wall on the TV, and a little character came down and sang, wrong way, wrong way.

"Hi, guys." His voice was wet, thick, shaky. It should've made him sound vulnerable, but to me, it only made him more intimidating. "Was thinking I'd take you to a movie."

Alec and I shared a look again. His car banged into a wall, and the wrong way, wrong way filled the room.

Dad wasn't a big movie goer. He wasn't a big anything, other than in stature. He went to work, ate his dinner, napped in his recliner, bickered with Mom and my older sister, and pretty much ignored me unless I got in the way of his routine.

"W-what movie?" Alec stuttered. I'm pretty sure it's the one and only thing he's ever said directly to my father.

Dad rubbed his hand over his chin. He'd recently shaved at the time. I remember thinking he looked so weird without the mustache. Almost like a completely different person, but still just as grouchy.

"There's a bowling movie. Thought we could check it out." He paused, fidgeting. "You two like bowling, right?"

Alec's dad had taken us bowling the week before. I see it now, but I sure as hell didn't then, that Dad was trying to compete a bit. For my attention, affection, adoration... I'm not sure. All I knew was at nine years old, I wanted more than anything to have time with my dad that wasn't filled with so much tense silence.

We turned off the Nintendo and got in the backseat of my dad's Crown Victoria. I bounced in my seat, eager to see whatever movie he'd take us to. He knew I liked movies, that I liked bowling. He was doing this for me, and I didn't know if or when that would ever happen again.

Alec was nervous. His mom said it was fine to

join us, but he was scared shitless by my dad. When we got to the theater, the ticket booth girl looked at us kinda funny when Dad told her what movie we were seeing. As soon as the movie started, I figured out why.

The Big Lebowski was not made with nine-year-olds in mind.

Turned out, bowling was a very, very small part of this movie. Many things happened at the bowling alley, and yeah, The Dude was in a league. But that's pretty much it. The rest of the movie made very little sense to me. I heard the f-word more times in those two hours than I'd heard my entire life. And there were boobs. A few of them.

Dad's face was the best, though. It went through so many color changes, and many times he'd rush to cover my eyes. I laughed when the audience laughed in the theater, most jokes flying over my head. But I liked The Dude. I liked The Dude's friends. I cried at the end. And Dad was my hero for taking me to a movie.

But he made both Alec and I swear on

everything that was holy... never tell our moms.

Over the years, I've learned to appreciate the cinematic masterpiece The Big Lebowski is. The humor, the direction, the tone, the camerawork...

But I'll always have a soft spot for it, even if it didn't have all that. It's the one secret that remains just between us guys.

THREE

"Waiting for me?" Tumbles asks, eyeing my untouched bowling shoes on the seat next to me. A six-pound bowling ball rests between her hip and forearm.

"I am a gentleman." Sure, I'll go with that. If only I had an editor for my actual conversations.

The corners of her mouth twitch. She swaps the shoes for her butt, setting them in my lap. I lose my head for a second. She smells like raspberries.

I drop the shoes, and they slap against the floor. "Ready for your second wave of embarrassment today?"

She snorts, leaning over to slip her own shoes on. "It really wasn't that embarrassing. Everyone misses the chair they're aiming for at one point in their lives."

My left foot sinks into the bowling shoe, squeezing my toes a little too much for comfort. "I don't think that's true."

"You've never fallen on your ass?"

"Didn't say that." I lace up and straighten, adjusting my cap. Gotta get a better view of those green eyes. "But I don't think I've missed my chair."

"Well, maybe no one ever pulled it out from under you."

She pokes my arm, and an unexpected surge of static snaps between us. She shakes her finger out, and I rub the sleeve of my ratty t-shirt. Literal sparks between us.

Her hands land on her knees, and she pushes to her feet. "You know how to use these things?" She points to the scoresheet. The campus bowling alley is apparently behind the times, still using a paper and pen instead of a large TV and automated scoring.

I take the three steps to look over her shoulder. The end of her ponytail tickles the crook of my arm, and I suck in a breath. Damn... Raspberries are quickly becoming my favorite fruit.

"Thought you were an expert bowler," I tease. "Don't know how to score a game?"

"Not without those little animals."

I raise a brow, and she flicks her gaze to me, a tinkle of laughter filling the small space between us.

"The alley back home had little jungle animals on the screen that kept score and cheered when you got a strike."

"What'd they do when you gutterballed?"

"I don't know." She slides into the seat behind the scoresheet and takes the pen. "Never happened to me."

"Sure." I grab a ball and hook my middle fingers and thumb into the holes. "So... where's 'back home'?"

"Georgia," she says on a sigh.

"You miss it?"

"I'm trying hard not to." She taps the pen on the scoresheet. "Um… this is super awful of me, but…" She makes a face. "I don't know your name."

Laughter rumbles my chest. "That makes two of us."

"We rock at this first date thing." A blush runs through her neck, and I wonder if she's worried over saying the word "date." That's exactly what it is.

I put her mind at ease and don't bring attention to it. "Landon Wangford."

She presses her lips together, her eyes drifting to the page as she slips my name into the first bowler slot. I lean over to see what she jots in the second slot, but she writes "Tumbles." As much as my heart seems to like that she's into the nickname I gave her, I still want to know her actual name.

I adjust the ball under my arm. Twelve pounds isn't that heavy, but it is when I'm holding it for a while. "Do I get to know yours?"

"Give me a strike." She nods to the pins. "Then we'll see."

Piece of cake. I wasn't lying when I told her I'm good.

I fix my hat, hold the ball in front of me, and strut to the line. The ball leaves my hand with a *pop!* And a throb shoots through my thumb. *Shit.* The ball dumps onto the lane, rolling so slowly two other bowlers get their balls down their own lanes before mine taps the pins.

They topple in slow motion, knocking down three and only shaking the last one before plopping into the back. At least it went straight.

The loudest and most obnoxious laugh fills the air, and I whip around. Tumbles covers her mouth, but a giant snort gets added into the mix.

If that isn't the best sound in the world, I don't know what is.

The corner of my mouth picks up, and I give her the bowler's walk of shame to wait for my ball. "My thumb got stuck."

"Uh huh…"

"It did!" I forget waiting for my ball and march toward the rack behind us. "You'll see." I test out a few of the balls before finding one with holes so big, King Kong could join a league. I pretend not to notice her as I walk to the line, but I notice. Her light wash jeans, the imprint of her phone in her back pocket, the pale blue of her fuzzy sweater, and the small strip of skin between that sweater and those jeans, peeking out every time she sits or stretches.

I'm going to get that name out of her. A split is almost a strike, and I'll present that argument as soon as I—

The ball wobbles out of my hand, dropping like it's made of metal. Again, it rolls so slowly I crouch, refusing to look at the source of that adorable laughter.

How heavy was that one? I knew it was heavier than thirteen, but I didn't think it was that bad. I can bench press more than a hundred for Christ's sake.

I get one more pin down. Good for me.

I straighten my shoulders. *Tip number twelve: confident*

without being cocky. Here it goes.

"Told you I was good." I blow on my fingers and rub them on my collar. She nods, clapping as I make my way to the scoresheet. My little 3 and 1 sit next to each other in small boxes, the 4 underneath. She's scoring beautifully, even though my first round was pitiful.

She knocks her shoulder against mine, sliding from her seat. "I have a feeling this will be very fun."

"Is the name deal still on the table?"

Her hip juts to steady the bright green six-pound ball she picked from the kid's section. "I might allow a split."

"You want something from me?" I offer. "Since I already gave you my name."

"Hmm…" She taps her chin, her chipped polish glittering under the lights. "You got some cash?"

I lift a brow. "You want me to pay you?"

Her eyes widen, wiping away her confidence in a second and replacing it with innocence. How does she pull off both looks so well? "No, no… I was… Well, I'm a little hungry, and that pizza smells really good."

She nods to the lane a few spots over, where a group of middle-aged women laugh and eat slices between their turns.

Duh. It's lunchtime. I'm one of those fools who forgets to eat all the time. And we are on a date.

Mental note: make sure the leading man in the short film takes care of the leading lady's food needs.

"You got a preference on toppings?"

"Ham and pineapple."

She's one of those. Luckily, so am I. And it's a hard sell here in New York.

I lean back, crossing my ankles in front of me. I wave her forward, silently agreeing to the terms. My brain goes a little haywire, picturing her rocketing that ball down the lane and blowing all those pins to pieces. I wonder how she celebrates… Is she a confident strutter? Does she have a touchdown dance? Will she clap and jump up and down? Does she fist pump the air, or act like it was nothing?

Every scenario has my blood pumping, my throat going dry.

A girl whose name I don't know has me all tangled up. Not sure if I mind. If anything, it's good research.

Her shoulders rise and fall with a deep breath. She takes three steps toward the line, pulling her arm back and then sending the ball.

It goes fast, that's for damn sure. Much faster than mine… and immediately into the gutter.

Now I'm the obnoxious laugher. It rolls through my gut, bursting from my lips with so much force my head tosses back. She smacks her forehead so loudly it echoes around us, and we draw the attention from the ladies a few lanes over.

"I'm nervous!" she says when she turns around. A smile lights her bright red face.

"Really want that pizza, huh? The pressure was on?"

She nods… at first, then shakes her head. She takes the

few steps to the ball return to wait for her six-pounder. "I…
Okay, this is my first date since leaving home and starting
school, and I really have no idea what I'm doing."

Could've fooled me. She has me wrapped around that
chipped polish finger already, and I get to my feet, hoping
my next move is okay.

I lightly tap her elbow, and her eyes meet mine. I gulp,
my throat suddenly not so dry. "I'm pretty sure we're just
supposed to… have fun."

The corner of her mouth twitches. "I am having that."

My breath seizes. I'm surprised I have enough air to
talk. "You know what would be more fun?"

"Pizza?" she says teasingly, but I see the hope
sparkling in her eyes. I'll get her that Hawaiian.

"And bumpers."

Laughter spills from her lips, and she stretches on her
toes, wrapping her arms around me. I'm thrown—this girl
is hugging me, and I'm hugging her back so automatically I
don't even realize it. But I don't want to let go, either. She's
so warm here, and her sweater is soft. Her hair tickles my
knuckles, her breath washes over my neck, and a string of
goosebumps runs up my head, and I swear every strand of
hair is on its end under my Beetlejuice hat.

She lets go first; I'm in too much shock to loosen my
hold until she does.

"Liz," she says.

"Huh?" My brain is stuck. On that hug. On that gap.
On raspberries.

Her skin is free of blush, and her confidence is back in all its glory. It's damn gorgeous.

"Liz. That's my name."

#8 BACK TO THE FUTURE

1985

DIRECTED BY ROBERT ZEMECKIS

My first girlfriend broke up with me during Back to the Future. I refused to make out while it was on. Apparently, if a movie was more important than kissing, I was not worth it.

She was out the door as Biff hit the manure.

And I laughed.

I was fifteen... so, I'll blame it on that.

I figured that if a girl was important, then she'd appreciate the importance of movies. Of stories. Especially ones as epic as Back to the Future.

Never did I think I'd find one important enough to pull me away from the screen. I pictured sitting on the couch, watching whatever was unfolding on the TV with a faceless dream girl beside me. Maybe one of my own films. Some day.

There are so many things to love about Back to the Future. The humor, the writing, the cinematography. The sequels, the fanbase, the acting.

But what struck me most, still to this day, was the ripple effect of one single action. The simplicity of one decision is actually complex. What would happen if two people didn't end up together, or if they did, but in a different way? Or how support and faith and confidence can make or break a person, a relationship, a family...

I hate to admit, I envied Marty McFly. He had a chance to see the "what ifs." Even better, he had a chance to change the life he ended up in.

Off one decision...

Everything can change.

FOUR

A bright yellow cab pulls up outside the bowling alley, its tires bumping against the curb. Liz and I both watch its movement, and I feel her actually deflate next to me.

"I wish I wasn't responsible." A frown turns Liz's lips, and then they form an imperfect O… like she didn't realize she was talking out loud.

My mouth quirks in the corner, and I lean against the brick building. "Why's that?"

"Because I'd call in sick or something." The wind blows a strand of her blonde hair across her forehead, and she swipes it away. "Fake a fever. A cold. The flu. Pretend to puke on the other line."

My shoulders shake with amusement. "You do that often?"

"No." She puffs out a breath so hard it rumbles her lips. "I'm responsible. So I will be clocking in. On time. Like always. Wishing I didn't have to work so I could just…" Her gaze drops to the ground, and her lips press tight together.

"Come on, Tumbles," I encourage. I want her to finish

her sentence. Finish that thought. It's most likely the same as mine, and I want confirmation. "You can say it."

She meets my gaze with narrowed eyes. "Well, now I don't know if I want to."

"I'll help," I tease, reaching for her chin. She lets me move it as I put on a high-pitched, slightly southern tone. "'I just want to spend more time with you, Landon.'"

She sticks her tongue out, the tip catching my thumb. I jerk it back, and she laughs. The echoes of that laughter will be singing me to sleep tonight for damn sure.

"Stop being cute," she threatens, and my heart rate skyrockets. "Or I will forget responsibility."

"I'd say no deal, but I like a responsible girl."

She throws me a wicked grin. "I'm very good with to-do lists."

"Stop."

"And spreadsheets."

"You vixen."

"And deadlines."

I hiss in a tight breath, and she slides in closer to me, her shoulders bumping with her small giggles. The sun ducks behind a cloud, bathing her in a blueish light. Her breath pushes out in a puff of smoke between us, mingling with my own.

I know we're saying our goodbyes. We've already established she has to get to work, and I'm set to help Jace shovel his grandmother's drive tonight. It's already been a long day—starting at three this morning for my morning shift before my ten o'clock class, then this lunch date with this unbelievable woman I met not a few hours ago.

Yet… there are not enough hours. I need more of them. I need at least one or a hundred.

I reach for her hand, touching her fingertips lightly with mine. She blows out another breath, this one a little growly as she takes my invitation and slides her fingers between mine.

"Stupid work."

"I agree."

"Maybe I will fake a flu."

"Test it out." I push off the wall to stand upright. "Give me your best flu-y voice."

She tilts her head but obliges. "I'm sorry, Hannah. I…" *sniff, cough, hack* "…can't come in tonight."

I raise a brow. "You're a theater major?"

She smacks my upper arm with her free hand. "I don't know what my major is, mister. But I can act, damn it."

"Maybe it's the smile." Not wanting to stop holding her hand, I nod to her lips. "Pull the corners of your lips down. Talk a little through your nose instead of your throat."

She makes a face like a dead fish. "Liiiike dis?"

I chuckle. "Much more convincing."

"If only I had the ability to lie." She sighs. "Or congestion."

"You allergic to anything? Maybe we could get you puffy."

"Ah, if only I was cool enough to have allergies. But alas…" She dramatically puts her hand to her forehead. "I am but a loser who is allergic to absolutely nothing."

"Damn. Guess there's no way out of this."

"Sadly."

"Even if you could get off work," I say, running my thumb across her knuckles, "I have responsibilities I have to get to as well."

"I would totally help you shovel a cute old lady's driveway."

"And I would let you."

She frowns and lets out another exasperated breath. "Stupid work."

"You said that already."

"And I mean it. Work sucks."

"I know."

Then she starts singing Blink 182, and I fall a little harder for her.

She's too damn adorable. Witty and fun and apparently into me, and I'm really into her… enough that I'm ready to pull her in and give her a whopping kiss.

Her tongue sneaks out and wets her lips, and I know she's thinking about it, too. We've just had one hell of a date; we both don't want to go, but we have to, and I'm trying to make time stop so I can have a minute to think. But the longer I'm in her presence, the more my brain *doesn't* think.

"Well," she says after I stand there and do nothing but

stare at her like a damn fool. "I'll see you in cl—"

I go for it. I mean, plunge face first into her. My lips catch the tail-end of her sentence and slide to the corner of her mouth. I think I'm kissing half-lip, half cheek.

Shit.

Panic ricochets up my spine, and I desperately try to recenter, but she moves at the same time and…

I find chin.

"Sorry," I sputter, but it's garbled against her lips—or her cheek or chin. I still haven't figured it out. Hell, I could be kissing her earlobe or forehead or any other part of her face at this point. Horror fills my chest, stronger than any Freddy Krueger film that kept me up for weeks, and I jolt back. Heat spikes up the nape of my neck, and her green eyes widen, blinking once, twice, three times.

If it weren't for the tingling in my lips, I'd wonder if what I just did would count as a kiss at all.

"Uh…" I mutter, running my hand up the back of my head, tipping my baseball cap enough to cover my eyes. If only it could cover my entire face. "I'll call you when I get home. Let you know I got there safe and all."

A pause. Three seconds at least. I don't dare meet her eyes.

"Okay." Another pause. An eternity of one. "Thanks for lunch."

"Yep."

Her hand slips from mine; I'd forgotten I even had a hold of it. I'm suddenly sweaty and cold all at once, and I only look up enough to watch her get into the cab. She offers me a wave, and I'm pretty sure I wave back, but who the hell knows. With the control I have over my body parts right now, I wouldn't be surprised if I accidentally gave her the bird.

Hell, I didn't wake up this morning thinking I'd be doling out a first kiss today. I would've prepared, that's for damn sure. Because even though I don't know much about romance, I know how important first kisses are.

And I just gave the worst one possible.

#7 SHAUN OF THE DEAD

2004

DIRECTED BY EDGAR WRIGHT

Alec's my best friend. It's really the only relationship I've had in my life that I appreciate.

Well, up until now.

So when I saw Shaun of the Dead, I understood one-thousand percent why Shaun made the decision he did in the end when it came to his buddy, Ed.

When it all comes down to it, your best bro always has your back.

FIVE

INT-Hotel lobby by Elevator: Night

LIAM and LAYLA *wait for the elevator at the hotel. Liam shakes like an earthquake because he knows damn well there's about to be a kiss. He needs to kiss her. But it's been too long since he's done the first kiss thing, and Layla is amazing, and he doesn't want to blow it.*

Layla casually leans against the wall near the elevators, her ~~green~~ eyes playful and casual and not at all like how ~~Landon~~ Liam is feeling, but it's so gorgeous he thinks, hell, I'll just go for it, so he does, and he completely misses, because Layla moves a little, and he only gets the corner of her mouth, and he is horrified.

LIAM: *I uh… sorry.*

He's sweating bullets. Layla taps the corner of her mouth, almost like she has no idea what the hell just happened.

LIAM: *Thanks for your number. I'll call you when I get upstairs.*

Let you know I got there safe.

LAYLA: Sounds good.

And he runs out of there like a fu8i9o0p-[;.

My fingers slip all over the keyboard, the car jolting to a stop in front of Jace's grandma's place.

"Brace yourself," he warns me. "I told her about Little Miss Fall on her Ass."

My jaw clicks, my back teeth chomping so hard against each other they slide off and take a chunk from my tongue. Alec gives me a pat on the shoulder from his spot in the back, but that's all the reassurance I get before we crunch our way through the snowy path to the front door. My laptop is a heavy weight in my hand, documenting the worst first kiss I've ever attempted in my life.

There was a part of me that thought if I wrote it out, put it into the script, it wouldn't be as bad as it was in my head. Maybe I did okay. Maybe I was hoping for fireworks or something since I've seen so many damn movies.

I'm very stupid sometimes.

I texted her when I got home. Like I'm a damn child reporting to his mother. My phone has been sitting in my pocket, silent as the dead. Why the hell would she use my number after that? No matter how good the date was—which was pretty high up there—I ruined it all with a mumbled apology against her lips.

"Shit," Jace hisses as his foot slides across the icy concrete steps. He snags Alec by the shoulder, but Alec's no steadier, and they both crash to the ground.

"Watch your step," I say through a laugh. Jace lobs a pile of snow in my direction.

"I'm going to kill that landlord," he grumbles.

"I'll help hide the body." Alec wobbles to his feet, using the side of the house to balance while he swipes his jeans off. We've been helping Grandma Carver with the snow and lawn maintenance since she moved in. She sold her house to pay for a giant investment mistake Jace made, and this duplex was all she could afford.

He thought she'd have a good landlord, or at least good neighbors who lived upstairs. But we're here at least twice a week to clear the drive and ice the walk. Jace calls it penance, but he'd do it for her even if she hadn't paid off his debt.

He gets to his feet, knocking on the front door with more force than is required. "Grandma? It's us. You decent?"

"Never!" Her contagious laughter muffles through the door. It's a good thing it snowed today; I need some Grandma Carver time. All my grandparents have passed, but even when they were alive, we weren't close.

Jace pushes in, slipping slightly on the landing. I take cautious steps, avoiding his exact pathing. A broken laptop is the last thing I need.

Heat blasts over me the second I cross the threshold.

Grandma likes to keep it a toasty ninety-five at all times.

"Did you tell Stephen you need the walk salted?" Jace asks, shaking his hair free of snow.

"Oh, I said I'll be breaking a hip any day now." Grandma wraps Jace in a hug. "He said he'd come out this weekend."

"It'll melt itself by then."

"Don't stress." She pats him on the small of his back, their height difference a full foot. "I don't have anywhere to be."

He meets my eyes over the top of her head. I'm right there with him. An unsettled annoyance bubbling through my chest erupts.

"I think I blew it with this girl I took out today."

Grandma Carver releases Jace, her eyes wide. Jace and Alec both look at me like I've lost my damn mind. Maybe I have. But I know Grandma loves to talk about our dating lives and is extremely bugged when we have nothing to say. This will keep her happy while Jace blows off some steam at her landlord.

"Is this with the girl from your class?"

"Yeah."

"You met her today?"

"Yes…"

"And you already think you blew it?" She chuckles, waving me off. "Oh, your sweet innocence. Sit your very exquisite ass next to my knitting there and settle in. This is going to be a while."

Jace and Alec hold in their laughter, but I catch Jace's "thank you" before disappearing into the small sitting room.

***

"I could feel his tongue in my intestines, Landon. Lord, I prayed for a swift death."

My face has been a steady inferno of heat. And it's not the radiator.

Grandma Carver huffs and adjusts my hands, her purple yarn wrapped around each of them. I sit like I'm calling a touchdown, resting my elbows on my knees and slowly losing feeling in my fingertips.

"I hope you had more class than that with Lizzie."

Lizzie... I like that. I'll probably steal it, if Tumbles doesn't mind.

That is, if I get to talk to her again.

"I kept my tongue to myself," I assure Grandma Carver. "Unless you count actively apologizing mid-kiss."

"I would've invited an apology after my first kiss with Jace's grandfather. Houy, he even played it up for me. Said he'd know his way around my lips since he'd been watching 'em all night. I thought it was romantic, obviously a line, but I gave in. Didn't realize he'd go tongue first."

"Or tongue only," I add, the heat in my neck turning up a few degrees more. Grandma Carver isn't shy—Jace gets that from her—but I didn't expect a full-blown recap of all the horrendous kisses she's experienced.

"Take it from a woman who knows... one bad kiss does not mean it's over."

"He got better, I take it?" Jace has a lot of aunts and uncles.

Grandma tilts her hands in a so-so motion, her knitting needles clicking. "Kissing isn't everything."

"I have a hard time believing that." Kissing scenes are imperative in *every* genre of film. And if I include the one I did today, this film will be DOA.

I have massive rewrites to do already.

"Oh, it's something." She tugs on the yarn, and it rubs against my knuckles. "Not *everything*. My husband may not have been good with his tongue up top, but he was fabulous with it elsewhere."

The red heat drains from my face, turns green, and lands in my stomach. "Grandma…"

"Don't get prudish on me. You want my advice, I know it. And I have good points here."

"And the details are necessary?"

She gives me a wicked look over her knitting needles. "Very."

'Details,' I find out, is not an accurate enough description. I know more about Grandma Carver's sex life than my own… and it makes me laugh and cringe in equal measure. I keep waiting for the point and searching for the advice part of it, but it's hard to find when she's telling me about a certain spot Grandpa Carver was determined to make work for her, but she was not interested, and to this day she can't look at the rocking chair the same way.

Thank Christ I'm not sitting in it.

"It was many years before we found a rhythm." She stops making the hand motion of the awkward shape of their tiny shower and how they had to stand and gets back to her knitting. "But when we did, it was more beautiful, more meaningful. Love works like that sometimes."

"Love?" I choke back a laugh. "Grandma, I met this girl not twelve hours ago."

"And you're tolerating an old woman's sex stories just to help you out." Her eyes sparkle behind her glasses. "You would've stopped me long before now."

"I didn't realize that was an option." I hold up the yarn. "You have me trapped."

"You're too kind to up and leave." Her focus lands on her knitting project. Looks like she's close to finishing, tying up some ends. "Kindness, curiosity, passion for your filmmaking, and that rear-end? You're a catch, Landon. Lizzie would be a fool to let one folly of a kiss stand in the way of spending time with you."

Damn. I wish she was my grandma. I've never had a family member give me such complimentary words, let alone a whole list of them. I'll even accept her obsession with my ass. "Can I adopt you?"

She humors me with a laugh, pulling her needles free from her project. I wonder if I can stop being her yarn holder, but I'll keep my position until she tells me otherwise.

"You call that girl tomorrow. Don't you dare text. And you ask her out again."

My heart stutters, and I check the window. Alec and

Jace look like they're packing it up and coming in within the next few seconds.

I lean closer to Grandma. "What if she says no?"

"She won't."

Her confidence is nice, but I don't believe it.

"If she does…?" I prod.

She levels me with a look that could kill, but it's also loving and kind, and it's one I don't ever see from my family.

"Then you put her on hold, call me, and I'll talk some sense into her."

I'm ready to argue more, but the sound of football talk enters, filling the room.

"…Giants have it this year." Alec throws his coat up on the hook, and Jace follows, both their faces bright red.

"Patriots. They take it every time."

"Not *every* time. Little guys got a shot."

"You just called the Giants 'little guys.'"

"Happy accident."

They stop when they catch sight of me playing the part of yarn holder.

Alec's brow furrows in concern, and Jace's mouth quirks in amusement. Both say in sync, "You okay?"

An hour ago, I would have answered with a resounding no. I'd let them know that the script is shit. I'm shit. Everything is shit.

But I take a quick look at Grandma, and I can't say everything is shit anymore. She managed to get some confidence to build inside me.

"Grandma thinks I should ask Liz out again."

Alec takes a spot on the rocking chair across from us. Grandma share a look, and she gives me a quick shush finger. Yeah, best Alec doesn't know the history behind that thing.

"It'd help the script, yeah?" Jace teases, leaning against the wall. "What not to do to get the girl."

Grandma bats a hand at Jace, which he dodges. "Don't talk about my second favorite like that."

Jace grins. "Second favorite? I'm flattered."

"Why?" She motions to Alec. "He's the one who should be flattered."

Alec's eyes widen, and a laugh bursts from my lips at Jace's indignation.

"I'm *third*? I'm your own blood!"

She quiets him, focusing her attention on her knitting, tying more knots and wiping it free from flyaway fuzzies. "What script is this, Landon? Not your zombie movie?"

I shake my head, adjusting my arms. They're starting to get those pins and needles. "Jace and I have a short film project."

Jace crosses his feet at the ankles, tipping his beer toward me. "Why you worrying about it now? We have all semester."

I lift my shoulder to scratch at where my hat meets my ear, but it doesn't reach the itch. "We have all semester to write, film, and edit it. I have to worry about it now because we need a script before filming, and filming will take the bulk of the time, and then there are edits and b-roll and—"

"Isn't this a group project?" Alec raises his brow toward Jace, who just innocently puts his hands up.

"You know him. All work, no play makes Landon a happy boy."

"You having trouble writing it?" Alec asks, freeing his blond hair from his beanie. "You wrote the last script in less than a week, and that's a full length."

I open my mouth, but Jace beats me to it. "He has to write a romance."

And my best friend tips his head back and laughs. It quiets when he catches the look of death from Grandma and myself. I might be moving up in the ranks.

"Sorry," Alec says, rubbing the back of his neck, his smile still very prominent. "I just know that isn't your thing."

"Exactly." I adjust again, and Grandma finally motions for me to take the yarn from my hands. "And the research did not go well today."

"Research…?" Jace says. "You mean your date?"

"Yeah."

"You didn't tell Liz she was research, did you?" Alec's face is dead serious.

"I'm dumb, but not that dumb." My eyes shift to Grandma Carver. We had this conversation, but she doesn't seem to mind the recap. I doubt the guys would make fun of me too hard in front of her. "The kiss was… bad."

"You kissed her?"

"Kinda."

"Did she laugh at you?" Jace asks around his own chuckle. "I've had that happen."

"No." But she should have. It would've made me feel better, I think.

"Well… don't write that in," Alec suggests. I'm already hitting the backspace button in my head. "It's not like you have to experience romance to write it. You wrote a zombie apocalypse, and I'm pretty sure you haven't lived through that."

I know this. I do. And if this was all about the script, I might be able to let it go.

But Liz is gorgeous and fun, and I want to spend more time with her. Not just look at her in class to see if she's looking at me. No girl has ever crept her way into the path I have set in front of me. Career first. Always.

But I'm thinking about the script sitting on my laptop, and that's not what I want to fix. And I realize with a shock that when Grandma Carver offered to sit with me and chat, I only brought up Liz.

Six

My hand has been clutching my phone like I'm Tom Hanks with a volleyball.

I've drafted twenty-one different messages to Liz, all not making the final cut when my inner editor came out. I've done apologetic to oblivious to teasing to cocky to goofy. I suck at all of them.

This is why I'm not a writer.

A defeated groan escapes me from the deepest part of my gut. One day I'll be able to do anything without researching the hell out of it first, but, in the words of Aragorn, it is not this day.

My finger jabs at the Xbox button, and I pick up the copy of 50 First Dates I borrowed from Jace. My collection is more of the Tim Burton variety and less Happy Madison.

Careful to not scratch the disc, I pop it from the case and tuck it in the Xbox. I grab my beaten notebook and one of many pens I stash around the apartment and settle in for a one hour, forty-six minute study session on how the hell to woo a girl after an awkward date.

Lucky for Adam Sandler, the girl forgets his worst

attempts. I make note of his blunders alongside his wins, my graph looking like my first drafts of anything—absolute shit.

All right, persistence is a good thing in this world. Looks like I need to suck up my pride and give her a call. Texting was my go-to, despite Grandma Carver's insistence. Should've known to listen to her in the first place.

I shut off the movie after the Beach Boys sing alongside the credits. The last notes I make are the writer and director so I can pick up more of their work. I've seen most of Peter Segal's stuff—Tommy Boy was one of my favorites as a preteen—but George Wing is new to me.

The movie wasn't bad, to be honest. Had me laughing. Didn't hurt that Liz has Drew Barrymore's cheeks.

With newfound courage from the study session, I scroll to Liz's name on my phone and mutter my opening line under my breath.

"Been thinking about your incredible talent. Three gutterballs even with the sides up. Thought I'd give you a call."

Funny, light, teasing, and plants the idea that I've been thinking about her. Which I have. Nonstop.

It's later, too. The movie gave the morning time to morph into mid-morning, and now I don't have to worry about waking her. Though I'm sure she's got a damn cute morning voice.

The phone rings in my ear, and I pace my small room. My strides are long, so I only get two in before I have to turn around.

"Hi, Landon." Her voice is bright and airy. I picture that adorable smile of hers, my name rolling off her tongue through that small gap in her teeth.

My brain misfires.

"Been thinking about your balls."

My feet stop dead, my neck filling with heat. I choke on my tongue as it fuses to the roof of my mouth.

"Really?" A small snort. "Me too. They never did manage to get that strike, did they?"

Relief acts as rubbing alcohol, dislodging my tongue and my gooey throat as it washes through me. "I got your name, though, Tumbles."

"And you refuse to use it."

"Tumbles fits you so well." Especially after gutterball number two. She threw her hands in the air and cried out, "*How?*" then slipped on her way to the ball return. Lucky my arms were there to catch her.

"I think I should be offended."

"Are you?" I start pacing again, running my free hand over my head. I'm hatless right now, and the lack of cotton against my palm throws me for a second.

"No." Her voice is shy and annoyed and teasing all at once, and I like how animated she is without being able to see her face. "I like it."

"Well, Tumbles, I'll continue to use it." Win. I have confirmation on the nickname. "You busy tonight?"

"Would you call watching 13 Ghosts busy?"

"I would definitely keep that on your schedule."

"I'd rather not." She makes a noise like a whoopie cushion, and she's talking again before I can process whatever she just did. "But guess who drew horror for their assignment?"

"Lucky," I mutter.

"What did you get?"

I don't even hesitate, though I probably should, considering she's unintentionally part of my research for it. "Rom com."

"So not fair."

"You got any recommendations? I could use them."

"Get a pen ready."

I laugh but follow her instructions. If I have another chance with her, I'm not going to risk screwing it up by not watching these.

"All right," I say when I'm ready. "Shoot."

"Princess Bride."

"Seen that one." I don't think there is a soul who hasn't. "But I'm up for a rewatch."

"My Best Friend's Wedding, My Big Fat Greek Wedding, The Wedding Singer... Oh! And The Wedding Planner..."

"I said rom com. Not wedding only—"

"Runaway Bride," she continues, completely ignoring me. "Bride Wars, Father of the Bride, Corpse Bride, Bride of Chucky..."

My pen stops mid-Chucky. "I know you're joking now,

but I'm massively impressed by how many movies you can name with the word 'bride.'"

"I can keep going with the wedding theme. Bridesmaids, 27 Dresses, Four Weddings and a Funeral…"

"I think I'm good." I toss the pen down. "You want any horror recs?"

She groans. "I'd rather not. I'll spend so much money on light bulbs."

"From watching movies?"

"From sleeping with the lights on." She lets out a deep sigh that goes straight to my head. What I'd give to sit next to her all night watching scary movies. "So are you writing, directing, acting…?"

"Writing and directing." I let out a humorless laugh. "Jace is useless unless he's in front of a camera."

"You don't have more people in your group?"

"I do…"

"And they aren't helping out?"

I run my hand over the back of my head again. Where did I put that hat? "They will. I don't mind doing it, really."

"But you prefer directing?"

"Hundred percent." The back of my knees hit the mattress, and I flop down on the unmade bed, staring at the ceiling. "What part are you playing in your horror project? You didn't say." Another note I'm using here… turn the conversation to her when possible. As much as I'd love to tell her about my sky-high dream to sit in a director's chair, I know I wouldn't stop once I got going. And I still haven't asked her out yet.

"Acting." She whoopie cushions again. "I'm not much of a writer or director type, but even if I was, they pointed at me and said, 'final girl.'"

"You get to be the badass Sidney Prescott."

"Who?"

I sit straight up. "Stop."

Her laugh filters through the phone. "Should I know?"

"Add Scream onto your watch list."

"No. No, no, no. That one kills Drew Barrymore. I can't see that."

My mouth twitches in a grin. Even I have to admit, I preferred seeing Drew in the movie I just watched. "Do you have any Barrymores to recommend in the rom com department for me?"

"Ever After."

"That's a rom com?"

"I laughed," she says, her voice defensive. "It's really good. Best Cinderella retelling by a mile."

I fall to the mattress and tuck my hand under my head, my nails catching on the loose thread in my top blanket. "All right, how about I stick with you during Scream, and then you stick with me during Ever After? Hawaiian pizza, Coke, ice cream…?"

I'm sweetening the deal, and I hope she takes the bait. I wouldn't mind watching a few movies with her, no matter the genre. But a horror? Horrors were made for date nights.

Make out *after* the credits roll, obviously.

"Another date?" she asks, and her voice pitches up an octave. Don't know if that's a good or bad sign.

"Uh… y-yeah. If you wan—"

"Yes," she rushes out. Then she clears her throat. "I want."

I stifle a victorious *wahoo!* My heart thuds so hard I can feel it in my empty gut. I should've had breakfast. "Great. Tonight?"

"Yes."

"Your place? Mine?"

"Yours…? But could you pick me up? I don't have a way to get to you."

"No problem. Text me the address."

"On its way."

The vibration against my ear tells me she's quick—and hopefully just as anxious to see me as I am to see her. "See you around seven."

"Six." She pauses. "I… I like to eat earlier than that."

And I like she says exactly what she likes. Makes this a whole lot easier on me. "Six. Talk to you later, Tumbles."

She says goodbye, and I hold the phone to my ear like a lovestruck idiot, listening to it click on the other end. My brain is all tied up, and my nerves are firing on all cylinders, and I need to move around, get all this adrenaline out of my body, even though I'm completely relishing in it.

I got the second date. Conversation was natural, and damn, am I feeling some chemistry. Now to just get on the right page with the physical part of things. I am not going to let her think I'm a lousy kisser, and I'm sure this is the last shot I'm going to get.

I push from the bed and tug my shoes on. Time to hit the RedBox for a matinee and some studying before I'm with Lizzie again. There's a movie I think might be perfect, and hopefully, they have it in stock.

What Women Want.

It better be an accurate title.

My sister and I don't have much in common. I'd put it all on black, actually, that we have nothing in common. In a sore attempt to get us to "connect," my mom suggested we watch a movie together. It was Halloween, '01. I was twelve, she was seventeen.

Mom and Dad went out for their annual Halloween poker tournament with their friends, which was basically an excuse to drink, smoke weed, and lose money. It was one of the few things my parents did together without fighting, so I'm not judging.

Elle and I were ordered to watch Beetlejuice and get along. We did neither of those things.

Twenty minutes after my parents walked out the door, Elle had a guy over, and she didn't have my qualm about making out during a movie. So I pulled it from the VCR during the opening credits and moved to my room. She might not want to watch, but I was fine with it.

Let me tell you, that Halloween, when I was twelve years old, I discovered something. Sitting on my banana chair, middle of my bedroom, doorbell ringing every so often, trick or treaters interrupting my sister's date, I fell in love.

Tim Burton hit something inside of me—the darkness, the comedy, the bait and switch... It was all there in that film. This goofy film that held so much meaning, and it was because of the way it was told. Apathetic father, loud mother, ghosts filling that void in an invisible teenager. The sets were odd, music was off-putting, yet there was wit in every line.

Beetlejuice was barely in the thing. And he was the star.

How did he pull that off?

That night, I filled my first notebook, scrawling note after note. Everything from lighting to camera switches to effects.

I enjoy movies... always have. This one... Well, this one was different. And the only thing that would've made it better was if Elle actually watched it with me.

would've made it better was if Elle actually watched it with me.

SEVEN

I rock back and forth on my toes, fixing my Beetlejuice cap. Liz said she'd meet me outside her apartment building, and after getting all the notes down, I take a deep breath and text her to let her know I'm here.

A door creaks open a few floors above my head, and I adjust my cap again. Not going to wuss out with this. I like her a lot more than anyone I've ever liked. It's rare for a girl to pull me from my work.

The squeak of boots against wet metal steps reverberates against my nerve-endings. I blow out a shaky breath, letting it cloud into the cold air. She's a brave woman to speed down the snowy staircase. At least one of us is brave; I hope it's contagious.

I crack my knuckles and open the passenger door. I kept the thing running so it would be nice and toasty for her. She's probably used to much warmer weather. I've got that all planned—this script in my head of how our night will play out.

Act one: hug hello, use the warm car to ask about her home life, pick up the pizza.

Act two: pop in Scream, sit next to her on the couch, offer a blanket, put an arm around her when she gets scared.

Act three: Ever After. Suck it up. She'll be so impressed with my lack of groaning. Take her home and make up for that disastrous kiss. Twice, if she allows it.

Slow and steady wins the race. I repeat the mantra when she appears at the top of the final staircase. Her blonde hair is curled around her face, a thick, knitted headband covering her ears to keep them warm. She's in a pair of jeans and a thick, bright pink coat, her cheeks already rosy from either the cold or just seeing me. I want to think it's the latter, because my cheeks are probably the same color, and it damn sure isn't from the cold.

"Hey," she says, her accent touching the y strong in her greeting.

And the script gets thrown out the window.

My feet move by their damn selves, taking me and my lips directly to hers. I cover her mouth, grasping her waist and tugging her as close as I can with that giant coat between us.

I don't miss this time. I don't apologize. I don't have much sense at all. After a small squeak of surprise, Liz melts into me, and I catch her, hold her up, keep her there. She tastes like mint, like she brushed her teeth right before coming downstairs. Fresh and clean and new… like all these feelings swirling inside my chest.

Research, movies, school… all of that disappears. It's just Liz—and I want to know who she is, inside and out, anything and everything, what makes her happy, sad, frustrated, excited…

It scares the hell out of me.

But I love scary things.

We part with a much-needed breath clouding our shared space. Her wide eyes search mine, searching for an explanation. My script is gone; so I go off the cuff, which is embarrassing honesty.

"Sorry." Can't seem to kiss her without apologizing. "My lips wanted to make up for last night." Heat runs up my neck, and I rub it away, hoping she doesn't notice. "They were pretty embarrassed after their performance."

Her green eyes glitter with pity. "They weren't that bad…"

"They also missed you." I toy with one of her curls cascading down her arm and tickling my knuckles. "They've been tingling since they said goodbye."

It's true, and I wouldn't admit it so boldly if my brain was working. I cringe at my own words, and Liz tilts her head, a smile spreading on her face.

"Awww."

"I didn't even practice that one."

She chuckles, then pushes up on her tiptoes. The material of her thick coat slides against mine, like an unrolled sleeping bag. She flicks her gaze to my hat, then spins it around so the bill isn't in the way.

This hat is my favorite; I wear it too often, and the thing is going to fade bad. I don't like people touching it.

Hannah, a girl I went on a few dates with a couple months ago, would take the thing and chuck it across the room. Like she was trying to be cute.

It wasn't. Not to me.

But Liz twisting it around, keeping it on my head but making it easier to reach my lips? It's the perfect combination of sexy and cute, and my fingers find her coat pockets, tugging her even closer. Her lips find mine… or mine find hers. I can't tell who kisses who, just that we're kissing each other.

She steps forward; I step back. My ass bumps the passenger door shut. She reaches around me, fumbling for a door handle to the backseat. I'm grateful I have one as we topple inside, lip to lip, limb to limb, tangled up. My mind is fuzzy and sober all at once, tapping my shoulder to make sure she doesn't take this the wrong way. This is not my MO. I stay on script—date three, if I make it that far, is when the make-out happens. After I know the girl for a bit. Know her enough to have my tongue down her throat, my hands under her hem.

"Hang on," I say. My body disagrees, and I only get my coat off, her coat off, before we're back at it. She's on top of me, her body closer without so much material between us. My hands skate over her goosebumped skin between her jeans and t-shirt. My backseat isn't big enough for this, but I don't give a shit. Her nails scrape through my hair, managing to pop my Beetlejuice cap free. And I let her. She can do whatever she wants.

"What's… what's your favorite color?" I ask, pausing to kiss her through the question. My brain won't shut the hell up, prodding and poking and making sure I do this right when it's telling me I'm doing it all wrong.

Her lips touch the corner of mine. "Red. What's yours?"

"Red, too." I'm not even lying. "Do you have a job?"

Her soft breath of laughter warms my cheek, her lips moving to my jaw. I realize too late that I already know the answer, but I'm too stupid right now to take it back. "Yes, but I want a different one."

"Me, too." I'll elaborate another time. Ask her more about hers another time. "Beer or wine?"

She props up on her elbow, meeting my eyes. "I don't drink. I'm eighteen."

I kiss her again. Just because I'm talking doesn't mean I don't want our lips to get bored between pauses. "Liar," I tease against the skin of her neck. Raspberries are definitely my favorite fruit.

"I don't drink *regularly*."

"Okay." I'll believe that. Despite the fact we're tangled up in the backseat of my car, she puts off the good girl vibe. "Coke or Pepsi?"

"Coke." She meets my lips for another searing kiss. "How… how old are you?"

"Twenty-three." I hope that doesn't scare her.

She raises a brow. "You don't look like it."

"I don't act like it, either," I joke, shifting a little so my back isn't killing me. She clings on, and my heart thumps under her palm.

"Why the questions?" Her gaze drops to my t-shirt, and her fingernail traces the design.

Though most of my blood is down south, enough goes north to answer her. "I don't want you to think I'm just trying to get in your pants." Though, I wouldn't be against that. "I want in your brain, too."

As the words spill out, I realize how true they are. Attachment isn't what I do. I haven't done it my whole life. My mom's love language is passive-aggressiveness, and Dad preferred ignoring problems rather than facing them. My sister has more snark and sarcasm than she does honesty, and when I left for New York, there was a boot mark on my ass.

The only things I'm attached to come from movies. Things that aren't real.

But my heart thumps under her palm, almost reaching out and latching on, hoping she'll take it. My throat dries in an instant, my breath locked in my lungs as I wait for her response. I don't know her well enough to know what she wants. If this is one of many flings she wants to experience in college. I may have just scared the living hell out of her.

The corners of her mouth twitch, and she stops tracing the words on my shirt. "You are getting closer to the keys that unlock both of those."

She taps my nose, and relief and joy collide inside me, and I roll her underneath me. A squeal of delight escapes her, and I love that it's snorted and real and much better than anything I've seen or read about. Her hands drift down, hooking on my belt loops. Mine rush underneath her shirt, swooping up her sides.

Her breath catches, but she looks me dead in the eyes. "Favorite food?"

I smile, and my lips become far too busy to answer her.

Eight

A snap goes through my back, cracking all the way up my spine and over my shoulders. I roll my neck, continuing to get all the kinks out before my next call comes through. For this being a busy call center, we have crappy chairs.

The line buzzes, and I answer with the typical script: thank you for calling. This is Landon. This call is being recorded. This job sucks, but I'm putting on a smile to help you with your problem, even though you'll be yelling at me in no less than five minutes because I'm not telling you what you want to hear.

There's a pause—long enough that I almost hang up. Wrong numbers happen all the time. But the best voice I've heard all day filters through my headset, and my finger slips off the drop call button.

"Is it really recorded?"

Have I had a genuine smile within these walls before now? Because it feels damn foreign.

"Sometimes," I admit, resting my elbows on my desk. "Is there a problem with your vehicle, miss?"

Lizzie snorts. "Only psychos own a car in New York."

"Careful. You're talking to one of those psychos."

"Good. Because I really am tired of walking."

I laugh. Out loud. At work.

I get a look from Ben on the other side of the partition, and I duck in closer to my computer and lower my voice.

"So, how many times did you call in before you got me?"

"Six," she admits, and I get butterflies. Damn butterflies. What is this shit?

"Didn't want to text?"

"I did. But I assume you are a dedicated worker who doesn't look at your phone while on the clock?"

"You'd be right." I haven't checked it, but that doesn't mean I wasn't tempted. "What's so important you couldn't wait?"

"Well…" she lilts, and I imagine her finger tapping away against her chin, her chipped polish pulling my attention. "I'm actually downstairs."

My brow furrows. "In my building?"

"Outside of it."

Those damn bugs in my stomach. "Because…?"

"Thought I'd surprise you. Maybe take you out. When do you get off?"

I check the clock, even though I know exactly how much longer I have in this hellhole. "Forty-two minutes."

She whoopie cushions her lips. "I will walk around the corner for food, then. You want anything?"

"You going for heroes or burritos?"

"Are heroes the same thing as subs? I'm still trying to learn the New York vernacular."

"Yes."

"Then heroes. Your drug of choice?"

"Italian."

"Any vegetables?"

"Olives, lettuce, jalapeños—"

"No kissing tonight. Hint taken."

"See if they have gum."

She laughs, making me laugh… and Ben stare.

"I better go. Just in case this call has been monitored."

"See you in forty-one minutes."

The line dies, and I sigh like a damn fool, leaning in my chair. These next calls will be the longest of my life but so worth it.

***

The bright lights of the sign reflect onto the street below, lighting up the green in Lizzie's eyes. She turns to me with a wide grin, lifting her shoulders.

"So… is this okay?"

I stick my hands into my coat pockets, taking a step to avoid the foot traffic turning the corner. "This is where you want to go, huh?"

She bumps into my arm. "Thought it'd help you with your short film."

A chuckle bursts from my throat. "It might."

She tucks her arm through mine, squeezing tight. An unexpected jolt runs under my skin, but I don't mind it.

Then we walk together through the doors of the Sex Museum.

I'm face first into a dildo. The lobby is a sex shop. Zig-zag black and white paint don the walls, dim lighting casting shadows around the room. Lizzie grins, her smile and raspberry scent turning my brain to mush.

"I've wanted to visit this place since I turned eighteen," she says, pulling her coat off and hanging it on the indicated hooks. "But Theresa is a butt, and she didn't want to come with me. And I wasn't going alone."

We step up for tickets, and she proudly shows her ID.

"Is Theresa your roommate?" I ask.

"And best friend. We grew up together."

"I've got one of those, too."

"A roommate and best friend?"

"Who are one and the same." Alec and I booked it out of PA the moment we graduated. He's headed for Broadway while I'm hoping to make it to LA.

"Would he come to the Sex Museum if you asked?"

I tilt my head back and let out a jolting laugh. "He would. But he would be very red the whole time."

"You're a little red yourself." She runs a nail up the side of my neck, and I jerk from the unexpected tickle spot. Huh… didn't know I had that.

"Well, the Sex Museum isn't exactly what I pictured for our third date."

"Fifth."

I raise a brow, and she presses her lips together. That

happens a lot; her blurting thoughts out like she doesn't mean to. And I fall a little bit more.

"I mean… we went bowling," she starts, ticking them off on her finger.

"And then watched movies."

"No…" She shakes her head hard. "We made out in the back of your car, and you gave me my first orgasm."

I choke on my tongue, and she gets a thrill from it. Yeah, I got handsy with her that night, and it was the most beautiful sight I've ever seen. Didn't realize it was a first for her.

Instead of continuing to count these dates I don't remember, I'm completely distracted. And it's not just the fact that we walk into a room full of sex toys.

"Is that true?"

"Hmm?" she hums, her head tilting at display of a sex doll.

I rub at the base of my hat, scratching at the line it's creating in my hair. "I… uh… gave you your first…?"

Her lips turn slowly upward, and she pushes on her toes, kissing directly under my jaw. "Yes. Not by my own hand, at least."

My brain is half muted by her affection. I've never been with someone so willing to touch in public—or in private, for that matter. So I have to pull my thoughts out of the muddied waters to keep the conversation going.

"I'm not sure how to process that."

She takes my hand, weaving her fingers through mine,

and we step up to the next display. It's a chair that looks like it has a lemon juicer smack dab in the middle. "Landon, it's a good thing."

"I know." My croaky voice is not convincing.

"I've had sex," she blurts, and I turn my gaze from the lemon chair to her. I can't tell if the pink on her cheeks is natural or from the lighting in here. "It wasn't great."

Amusement loosens my chest. "Obviously."

She playfully knocks into my side, then we walk to the other displays. I'm looking, but not really taking in any details. I'm surrounded by pictures of naked bodies, but all I can focus on is the woman completely covered beside me.

"What about you?" she asks after a minute.

"Huh?"

Her brows rise. "Sex." Her hand twitches in mine. "You've had it?"

I can't stop my laugh. I laugh a lot around her. "Yes."

"Don't laugh at me. It's a valid question."

"Because I am a dreadful kisser?" Might as well bring that up since we're going there.

"You are definitely not that."

Heat rushes up my neck, and I resist the urge to rub my hat. "I had a horrible opening act."

"But you killed it at the encore." She swivels in front of me, pushes up on her toes, and pecks my lips. Before she gets too far from me, I press a hand at the small of her back and keep her there for a few more of those kisses.

She wiggles her nose against mine, and I feel more of

those damn butterflies as she drags me into the next room. We wander through the museum. She points things out just to embarrass me, so I do the same, and pretty soon we're the immature twelve-year-olds laughing at every penis and boob display and annoying other patrons.

"There's a boob bouncy house around here somewhere, and I am not leaving until we play in it." Liz skips down the steps, and the lights turn from white to red.

"It's gotta be around here somewhere," I add as we pass a sign displaying CARN-O-RAMA. It's a long, skinny hallway, and a clock that displays a countdown timer ticks away over a door.

"Maybe through there," she says, leaning against the wall. Her hand is still latched with mine. I'm sweaty, but I don't give a shit.

She tugs me closer, and I eye the clock—three minutes—before resting my free hand over her head. "Wanna make out?"

"Always."

We laugh, but I only give her a chaste kiss. Her knee knocks against my leg, and I get distracted by a curl at the nape of her neck, too little to get tucked into her ponytail.

I clear my throat. "Can I ask you a non-sexual question?"

She snorts. "I wasn't meaning to only talk sex with you."

"Sure. That's why you brought me here."

She wrinkles her nose, and I'm tempted to grab it.

Pretend I've got her nose. Put it back. Kiss her senseless.

"You going to ask me or tease me?"

I squeeze her hand, running a thumb across hers. "What do you want to do?"

Her head tilts, smile twitching. "Right now?"

"In life." Don't know why it's hitting me. Why her answer means so much to me. If it'll align with mine… why I want it to align with mine. "You're in an advanced theater class. Is that your major?"

Her teeth sneak out and pull at her bottom lip. That small gap gets to me, and I almost kiss her before I get my answer.

"I haven't declared a major. I'm only a freshman."

A small chuckle shakes my shoulders. "I feel like I had my major declared when I was twelve."

"You knew that early, huh?"

"A hundred percent." I swallow hard, but the words spill out despite my effort to keep them back. "I started writing my first script around then. Took a long time to get it done. But I filmed a lot, forced Alec to participate."

"He's your best friend-slash-roommate, right?"

"That would be him. He was not always willing, but I say it got him over his stage fright."

"You're such a good friend."

I bop her on the nose. "I am."

"I wasn't being sarcastic." Her eyelids flutter downward as she looks at our feet. "I love that you know what you want. I'm still looking."

"Any ideas?"

She lifts a shoulder. "I'm in no hurry." Her eyes drift up to mine. "I take it this short film is a big deal for you, then?"

I nod. "The grant would be life-changing. Career-forming. Dream-fulfilling."

Her smile widens. "I could sabotage my group for you."

My shoulders shake with amusement. "I appreciate the offer, but I think I want my talent to win out."

"Good call."

The clock ticks to zero, and the door clicks. I push off the wall, giving her space. A rush of cold air swarms me. I didn't realize how comfortable it was being warm.

A worker greets us, and then takes us into a theater-style room. We're given instructions on the boob bouncy house, the dick-jerking contest, and other fun carnival games. I'm unsure what we're in for in the next room, but the excitement in Liz's eyes is damn contagious.

We watch a short video on sex in public places throughout history. Liz scoots close to me, her head dropping on my shoulder. I kiss her forehead completely involuntarily, almost like it's programmed in me.

After the video, we are invited into the carnival room. The door opens to a very reflective hallway with bright lights. I'm glad I don't get motion sick, or I don't think I'd make it through.

"There it is!" She points like a kid finding their favorite

character at Disneyland, then tears my arm out of its socket to get us in line. There aren't a ton of people here on a weeknight, so we're up next. She grabs my shoulder for balance and rips her shoes off.

Once the group in front of us are out, she bounces in, stomach first, rolling off a boob bigger than a beach ball.

Her laughter filters out to me. I can't wait to join her, diving in and slipping on the first step. I plummet, getting a mouthful of nipple before rolling to my back.

"Slippery."

She laughs and struggles to her feet. "Need help up?"

"Maybe." I reach for her, and she uses all her strength to get me standing. As soon as I'm stable enough, she starts bouncing.

"How old were you when you first saw one?" she asks through a smile so large it will keep me up all night.

"A boob?" I start to bounce, my socks slipping on the landing. "Nine."

"*Nine?*"

"The Big Lebowski. My dad took me. Realized way too late there was nudity."

A joyous, unfiltered laugh pops from her mouth. It's the greatest sound in the world. "That rug really tied that room together."

My heart stutters. It might have even fallen out, bounced over a boob, and landed in her palms. She just quoted one of my favorite movies—a very obscure one.

I jump toward her, ready to catch her around the waist,

pull her to my lips, and keep her there until they kick us out.

But the force of my weight knocks her backward. A squeal escapes her, and she disappears between two boobs. Her bright pink socks stick out from the nether, her toes wiggling.

"Tumbles?" I ask through a laugh.

"The cleavage ate me!" she says, her voice muffled by a pair of inflated breasts. I wobble over, peeking into the small space she slipped into.

"You need help?"

"I'm stuck. Seriously, I can't get out." Her eyes are wide in panic, but her smile is still glued on her face. Laughter I've never felt before shakes my entire body, making it difficult to get a good grip on anything to help her out.

I wrap one hand around her dainty ankle, then hold on to the only thing that will get me traction—the nearest nipple. She's not heavy, not light, and her jeans make a *zoosh* as I pull her out of the cleavage cave. Her inner thigh smacks into my knee, and I let go of her ankle and reach for her hand.

She takes it, sitting upright, breathing hard, matching my breath and laughter.

"There should be a warning," she gasps. "Boobs may eat you alive."

I don't hold it back anymore, taking her by the neck and kissing her lips hard—well, as hard as I can while smiling like a damn idiot. She swings my hat around so the bill isn't in the way, and then meets my every move with just as much fervor.

After ten minutes of making out in between a set of knockers, we're asked to leave the bouncy house. I think with any other girl, I'd be embarrassed to get caught like a couple of fourteen-year-olds. But with her, I'm disappointed we didn't get more time in there.

NINE

INT-Hotel Lobby: Late Afternoon

Liam is lost in thought, the lobby music playing around him. He's watching Layla work behind the front desk, her eyes twinkling every time they meet his.

He twitches. Fiddles with his hands. Nervous. Confused.

It's been three days. It can't have happened that quickly, and he knows it.

But he still feels it.

Liz's chin plops onto my shoulder, the scent of raspberries now in every fiber of my apartment.

"Whatcha doing?"

A smile finds me, and I shut the laptop and turn. She's a much better view than my work in progress. "Writing the script."

She perches on my lap, straddling me in my pitiful

kitchen chair. It's the one that came with the fold-up card table that Alec and I use for our "dining."

"Which one?" Her butt is bony as hell, digging into my thighs, so I adjust her, cinching her closer.

"Rom com."

She sticks out her bottom lip. "Still no name for it, huh?"

"Nothing yet." But it's almost completely written, so that's a plus.

"Hmmm." She taps her chin. Her nails are free of polish and have been after our fourth date when I noticed it missing. "Front Desk Romance, Keys to my Heart, Love and Room Service..."

I snort, shaking my head. My reaction doesn't deter her.

"Heartfelt Reservations, Love's Lodging, A Room with a View... of *Looooove.*"

"All winners." I tickle the crook of her knee—one of her many ticklish spots I've discovered in the month we've been seeing each other. She jerks against me, her body so comfortable on me and my body so comfortable with hers that they lock at the bellybuttons and her lips automatically drop to mine.

It's heaven. And I know I should ease her off my lap, get to work on the project. Recording needs to start yesterday. My group is getting antsy. Audrey keeps asking if I want her to take on some of the writing—or look over it. But I'm still in the drafting stage... and my fingers have been too busy to find my keyboard.

I shift us to the couch, and she giggles and trips the whole way. That's the best part of her—she's always fun. Our asses hit the cushion, and my lips miss hers by a few inches, but she doesn't seem to mind. For every awkward kiss, I make up for it with a thousand good ones.

"Maybe you need some inspiration," she says, wiggling her nose against mine.

"This is inspiring," I say along her neck. Her laughter vibrates my lips, and she pushes me slightly.

"I was thinking… My Big Fat Greek Wedding."

I groan, slumping in the crook of her neck, my forehead resting on her shoulder. "I'm rom com-ed out."

"You want to get that grant, don't you?"

I groan again. Yes. I want it more than anything. Need it to prove that I'm actually good at this. My zombie script is just waiting for funding.

She takes my grumblings as a yes and hops from the couch, leaving my skin in a rush of cold air. I watch her cute ass as she wiggles and dances, popping in the movie and grabbing a blanket. She's certainly made herself at home at my place. Not that I mind.

She snuggles in close as a very Greek soundtrack plays through the speakers. "This one is hilarious."

"I'm sure it is."

"And it's got Joey Fatone."

I raise a brow, and she drops her mouth open in mock shock.

"Joey… from N'Sync."

"Of course."

She shakes her head. "For a theater nerd, you have no culture."

"N'Sync is culture?"

"Yes." She plucks my hand from the back of the couch and settles it on her shoulder. Her head lands on my chest, and I tap the beats of my heart against her arm. I'm not used to such close quarters so naturally. Don't remember the last time Mom and Dad gave me a hug—or a high five, even. But the last month with Liz has changed me into this have-to-touch-her-in-some-way guy, and I want more of it. She's touchy-feely, and it's melted away all my antisocial tendencies. At least with her.

"You aren't paying attention at all," she accuses after a few minutes, thrusting her hand toward the TV. "This is comedy gold and not a crack." She pokes at my mouth, and I playfully bite at her. A wrinkle appears above her nose, and she levels me with a glare.

"I'll watch. I promise."

She presses pause and sits up. "What has got your mind so occupied?"

Her. Always. "Nothing."

"Lies."

I let out a sigh, and she waits for me to get it out. I've learned with Lizzie to give in with honesty. I'm heavily rewarded when I do.

"Do you come from a family of huggers?"

Her head tilts in the cutest way, like a puppy wondering why she's not getting any treats. "I guess… Why?"

I lift a shoulder. "Curious."

"*Why* are you curious?"

I offer her my hand, and she instantly takes it. My fingers tumble and toy with hers, my thumb running over each and every one of her polish free nails. "Guess I'm wondering if you are touchy with everyone…" I swallow hard. "Or if I'm special."

"You're special." She drops her gaze to our hands. "Does it bother you?"

"Hell no." I'm glad my answer is quick. The smile that lights her face is worth the rush. "I just… Well, I hope I'm doing okay."

"What do you mean?"

I scratch at the back of my head, my fingers digging in the hole of my hat. "I come from a family of… not huggers."

"Are you worried your hugs are bad?" She does her whoopie cushion impression. Then she leans in and kisses the tip of my nose. "They are the best hugs in the world. Silly."

I kiss her nose back, following her lead like I always do. "It's not that. Or *only* that." I gesture to the TV. The protagonist and her father are in the car, the pause button creating an unflattering look for both actors. "These movies… writing the script… I'm getting the feeling that touch is a big thing in a relationship. And for you… Well, I just hope my touches are big enough."

A slow smile spreads across her face, and heat rushes through my neck. I toss my head back, covering my eyes with the bill of my hat.

"Gah… forget everything I just said."

"I will not." She takes my cap off, tossing it to the side of the couch that has been very lonely for the past month. "Landon, you don't need to worry." Her fingers tap against mine—small, barely-there taps. "I like this touch." She guides my hand to her knee. "This one." Then she slides it up her thigh. "Definitely this one."

A laugh tumbles from my gut, and I squeeze her ass, coaxing her onto my lap. Her shoulders shake with her amusement.

"That one, too." Her smile falters but doesn't disappear. It only takes on a more serious joy, less playful. "I know we come from different roots, and we probably express feelings differently. But I like how you express them to me. Whether it's this…" She wiggles her butt on my thighs, tucking in close to me. "Or with this." She taps my lips, then her eyes skate to my forehead before she lightly taps my temple. "Or with letting me know what's going on in here."

I need my laptop. She's giving me writing gold. But my fingers wrap around the crook of her knees instead, and I cinch her to my waist. Love is on the tip of my tongue, but I don't know if it's real yet, so I don't let the word sneak out.

"I like you."

She snorts. "I would hope so."

"More than other people."

"That's good."

"People I've known for a long time."

"Keep talking."

My hands slide from her knees to her thighs. There's a stain on her jeans from the salsa we had earlier. She swiped it up with a finger and didn't give it another thought. And another string of my heart latches onto her.

"I don't want to see anyone else."

"Ever?" she teases, and I pinch her lightly.

"Can we make this official, please?"

"Yes," she blurts. "I sort of made it official in my head weeks ago."

So did I, but my words don't get out. My brain says kiss her, and I do what my brain tells me. Most of the time.

I wrap my hand around the back of her neck and pull her to me. Our lips collide, and she grins like hell through it, which makes me grin like hell, and I hate that I've turned into a lovesick pup over the course of a few weeks, but I hate most that I don't hate it. Not even a little bit. Not even at all.

And now I'm quoting lines from rom coms, damn it.

Her torso zips up mine, her breasts crushing against my chest, her arms wrapped tightly around my shoulders, leaving mine to roam her ribs, her sides… run under her shirt and skate across her incredibly addicting skin.

Touch is good. How did I never realize how good it was?

She tugs at my collar, begging to free me from the material. I let her slide it over my head, only parting our lips briefly. Now her hands are the wanderers, tracing and tickling. She manages to make me hot and cold all at once, and it's getting more and more obvious how blind I've been to romance. How can anyone scoff at the idea of this?

I yank at her shirt, and she raises her arms, allowing me to get it off. We've gone this far before. I've touched her in places I know she doesn't let just anyone have a go at. But there is something deeper pulling at me this time. Something I think I can put a name to, but again, the word won't manifest in my clouding mind. Her tongue reaches for mine, and I meet it, let it thrill and wake up every sense in my body. My fingers find the clasp on her bra, and she lets me fumble for a good five seconds before helping me out.

"One day I'll get it," I say between our lips.

"This one sucks, even for me." She wriggles, her mouth contorting with the cutest concentration. "I got it for a discount, and I really think it's because of the hooks."

After a couple more attempts, she growls and just yanks it over her head, the cups smacking me in the face on their way up.

"Sorry," she says. "I'll kiss it better." She presses her lips to my nose.

"All better."

"I hurt my boobs, too." She playfully pouts, and my smile is equal parts excitement and amusement. "Help a girl out?"

I kiss up and down and across every inch of her gorgeous chest, teasing and sucking and playing while she giggles and squirms and moans.

This was another thing I didn't know was possible—having fun while being intimate. I certainly had fun, don't get me wrong, but my bedpost isn't exactly full of these kinds of fun moments. Liz and I haven't made it to the bedroom quite yet. I'm unsure if I'm waiting for a green light or for her to make the first move. Or if I was simply waiting to make things "official."

Now that I have the exclusivity thing done, maybe it's time to...

She nibbles at my earlobe, and holy hell, my brain is no longer. I surge to my feet, taking her with me. I find the nearest wall and slam her against it, bracing myself with one hand and holding her up with the other. Her smile is gone. So is mine. Yet, I've never felt so happy in my life.

"I... I *really* like... these touches." Her voice is breathy and electrifying. I get why that's used as a descriptor—the spark. It's more like a lightning bolt. I wouldn't be surprised if every hair on my body was ramrod straight.

I give her more of those touches, pressing her hips to the wall, pinning her underneath me. Her bare skin isn't foreign, but that doesn't mean it hasn't lost its strength. In fact, I think the more I hold her, the more powerful the feeling becomes.

She's twisted my insides around and around, and I rely so heavily on logic, but there is no logic to this. It's been four weeks. Four. How has a woman wriggled in and changed everything in such a short amount of time?

Her nails trail fire down my back, and I'm not going to ask myself any more questions. I will ask her one.

"Tumbles?" My breath washes over her neck, creating goosebumps in its wake. I pepper kisses along the path, from her collarbone to her shoulder. "I want to ask you something."

She shifts, her head rolling against the wall, her ponytail getting looser and more frayed. "Go right ahead. But I don't guarantee a coherent answer."

As much as it sucks to pull back, I force myself to. I'm still holding her, but my hips slow to a standstill, my hand pausing in its exploration of her ribs and breasts. My mouth is mad, but it'll have to wait before it latches on to her again.

"I need a coherent answer."

She pouts and lets out a rumbled sigh. "Better get out from between my legs, then." And without thinking, I twitch, and she growls, then drops her head on my shoulder. "That is not going to help the brain to brain."

I chuckle, and she growls again from the movement. I'm surprised I'm able to keep my head on enough to find it amusing.

She slithers from my hold, which isn't an easy feat, I'll give her that. My fingers pop and strain as I release my hand from the wall.

I let out a harsh breath through my nose, jaw clenched. Damn, I hope I don't mess this up. Rom coms usually fade out at this point.

She blinks, her green eyes a little hazy, yet still alert. Her lips slightly part, letting me see that adorable gap.

I love that gap.

"Can I take you to my room?" It's not specific enough, and I know it. I kiss her forehead. "I'd like to do unspeakable things with you."

"You're amazing." Her lips press together. She didn't mean to say it, but I'm so glad she did. "Yes, please."

"I don't know if I have a condom…" I reach around for my wallet, knowing damn well there's not one in there. And if there is, it's dusty as hell. It's almost comical—the emptiness when I open it up. In a movie, a moth would fly out.

"That might be a problem."

I meet her gaze, pissed I didn't prepare. "There's a gas station on the corner."

"I could go for a walk."

"Or Alec might have one." It's a long shot. If I was rooming with Jace, then there would definitely be a supply around here.

"I'll check the bathroom. You check his room." She playfully claps her hands together. "And break!"

She has to be so cute. I kiss her, long and hard, before she shoves me away and practically sprints for the bathroom. "Search, damn it!" she calls out, her voice bouncing off the walls. I run a hand through my hair and duck into Alec's room.

I don't know where the hell they'd be if he had some. He's a tidier person than I am, and I realize with sudden dread that my room isn't exactly romance ready. I peek out from his room, making sure Liz is still occupied. Her long blonde ponytail pokes into view as she digs around the bathroom drawers.

I dive across the hall and speed clean like my life depends on it. I'm notorious for leaving my socks everywhere and anywhere, and there are at least six different ones on my bed. I chuck them into the basket and fluff the comforter, praying she doesn't care if the bed isn't made like a hotel. My script notes are strewn across my desk, DVD cases piled on top of my nightstand.

I have the room of a fourteen-year-old.

A snort comes from the doorway, and I turn, meeting her gaze with a guilty grin.

"You okay, Landon?" she teases, hip jutted, shoulder against the doorframe.

"Yep."

"Worried I'll judge the state of your room?"

"Absolutely."

That wrinkle above her nose appears, and her shoulders bump with her silent laughter. "That's cute."

"Cute?" I grimace. "Cute is not the word I want."

"Thoughtful?"

"That's all right, I guess." I take a step toward her, forgetting the mess. "Sexy is better."

"Oh Landon, you have no idea how sexy it is when you are cute."

Her eyes sparkle when she teases me. I hope to God I see them sparkle every time we're together.

I get close enough to snag her waist and drag her against me. "I guess I'll have to accept cute."

"Cute is not bad." She leans back from my descending lips, putting a box between us. I kiss cardboard. "And lookie what I found."

Never thought I'd find the sight of Trojan so beautiful. "Hallelujah."

She moves the box, wrapping her arms around my shoulders. I press her bare skin against mine once more, loving that we just had this little adventure both topless, and it didn't even faze her. She kicks the door shut, and I reach behind her to lock it, the click sounding in my ear and buzzing every nerve ending in my body.

I'm about to take her. Sex is too soft a word for what we're doing, yet I still can't make my brain say what we're actually going to do. *Too soon, too soon, too soon*, is all it chants. But my heart says, hell no, it's waited too long to feel this way.

Her back hits the bed, and I come down on top of her. Our kisses have turned from teasing to passion in less than half a second, my tongue raking across hers, our breaths mingling, our skin on fire.

A wave of heat ripples up my spine and the back of my head when her thumb pushes the button on my jeans. I cradle her face, keep her close, telling her with only my lips and not my voice to keep going, keep touching. Teach me how to do romance, because I'm a very determined student.

That word prods in my mind again when my jeans flop around my ankles. I kick them away, then hurry to free her from hers. I'm much better with them than I was with her bra, shucking them from her legs in one fell swoop. Her panties are pink, and they didn't match her bra, which was white, and the side of my mouth quirks at the detail. Movies have wardrobes and actors have scripts, and this was unplanned and unexpected for both of us tonight, and we're still moving forward. I like it so much I can't help but fall onto her, eliciting a tiny, "oof," from the thick of her throat.

"You're so damn beautiful," I say, clutching her shoulders.

"Thank you." She wiggles her nose against mine. "You're easy on the eyes as well."

The word is on the tip of my tongue, so I shut it up and kiss paths across her lips, the apples of her cheeks, her jawline, the crook of her neck, down to her breasts—I spend a lot of time there—and over her bellybutton. She lets me love her body like love is something we're capable of feeling this soon.

"You, please," she says, her voice deeper, raspier. She grapples at my arms, urging me to hover over her. "I need you."

"I'm right here."

"You know damn well what I mean, Landon."

I laugh at her curses, settling in where she wants me. She digs into the box she found and pushes the condom into my chest with one finger. I try to be suave and tear it open with one hand and my teeth, but I miss on the first— and second—shot.

When I'm finally sheathed and ready, I meet her eyes one more time. "It's okay?"

She glares, like I'm taking too long, and grabs my ass. "I am not a patient person."

"I'm quickly finding that out." I push against her hands just to watch that frustrated knit in her brow. I get what she means—cute is sexy.

"Landon…"

I chuckle and stop my torment. We meet together, and the playfulness isn't gone, but it sure quiets. And I wish I could say I last all night. That I spent every waking second pleasuring her, feasting on her body and her heart and weaving my way into sex icon status.

I don't. I last about two minutes. Maybe three.

But Liz? She lasts ten seconds. And it's the most gorgeous sight I've ever witnessed.

We lie in the dark, the moon spread out across my sheets. I find a stray sock under my pillow and chuck it into the unknown darkness, jostling Liz resting on my chest.

We're uncovered, and it's not our nakedness that makes me feel completely vulnerable.

That word… the big one. The one I know I shouldn't have a name for, but I do, keeps rolling around my tongue, begging to be released. The L and the V hit my top teeth while the vowels tickle my uvula. I clear my throat, force my lips together. I will not ruin this perfect moment with too-soon declarations.

Her fingertips caress my chest, playing with the hair, tracing patterns. She's writing something in cursive along my skin. Her name, I think. Maybe mine. There's definitely an L.

I take that hand in mine, weave our fingers together.

And I squeeze it. Twice.

#5: UP!

2009

DIRECTED BY PETE DOCTER AND BOB PETERSON

This movie was an assignment, and I'll be real... I hate assignment films. When I'm forced to watch something, look for something specific, type up an essay or whatever on the aspects of that film the professor was looking for... yeah, I don't go for that. I hate it. I want to discover all the good and the bad myself. Go in blind.

So when I sat down to watch this one, I was in a damn bad mood. I had to pay for it, since it was still in its theater run. I'd gotten off a rough shift. Got yelled at most of the day. Was piss poor and too tired to think.

But this was the final assignment. We were studying montages. Footloose was on the original syllabus, but the professor scrapped it the second he saw UP! Told us to get our asses to the theater and watch that one.

Footloose would've been good. I knew that

montage like the back of my hand. I was cussing out my professor during the trailers.

Don't worry... I apologized for all the f-bombs after that first ten minutes.

It was the one and only time I recall being so wrong. The montage alone was well worth the ten-fifty, and when I got home, I was so taken with it, I couldn't sleep.

Montages—powerful ones—make the viewer feel with only visuals, only soundtrack. No dialogue, no need for that. The actors get to shine, and the director really gets to show off what is meaningful.

To elicit such strong emotions with no words is the goal of every filmmaker. And they knocked it out of the park.

I was humbled that day. Put in my damn place.

And I learned that words don't always need to be said to express how I feel.

TEN

The next two months fly by and yet are the slowest in history. The mystery box of condoms were courtesy of Jace, who apparently stashed them in my place when he saw I was spending more time with Liz than on my computer. He brought it up, very smug-like, when he noticed the box missing. I didn't confirm or deny, but I'm sure my face did.

Liz's, too, since she was cuddled into my side on the couch.

I finish the script. It's very rough, and I change it daily, but at least our group has started filming. Between that, school, and work, my free time is all Liz every day. We watch a lot of movies. Well, we *try* to watch a lot of movies.

We talk a lot. Tease a lot. Whether naked or clothed, we always seem to have our hands all over each other and our mouths running with whatever we have in our minds. Mundane conversation about how my day is becomes foreplay. Talk of her interests and how she grew up becomes afterplay. Teasing becomes during play, and it's the best play of all.

She loves my hats, stealing them and wearing them,

swiveling them around my head, batting at the bill, calling me sexier Luke Bryan, which is ludicrous, but I let it slide. I revel in the thought of her wearing one of my hats, seeing it too big on her head, or pulling her ponytail through the gap in the back. I've even allowed her to swipe the Beetlejuice one, almost begging her to take it from my head and settle it on hers.

I'm tempted to just ask her to live with me, since she's here all the time anyway, but it's too soon.

All too soon.

I keep telling myself that, but my damn heart won't listen. It's taken the non-verbal approach with the L-word whenever Liz and I are together. I squeeze her hand twice, two pumps in quick succession.

Love you.

It's what I'm saying, what I mean, what I feel, but no way in hell is it coming out. Research has proven to be pretty unanimous in the "I love you" coming at the right time.

There is still so much I don't know about her. There's a shit ton she doesn't know about me.

But my heart doesn't care. It loves her anyway.

Her hand slides in mine automatically whenever we're together. She makes an expression, and my fingers squeeze twice. She whoopie cushions those lips... *pump, pump.*

She quotes Tim Burton, and my hand can't react quickly enough, squeezing twice to the beat of hummingbird wings.

I don't know if she thinks I have turrets or a tic. She doesn't mention it. Only squeezes back once. Tight. Strong. I pretend she's reciprocating.

I'm a fool.

And I don't care.

ELEVEN

My phone buzzes against my hip, and I ignore it, even though I'm damn sure it's Liz. I don't *want* to ignore it. I wish I could abandon this project and spend all my free time with her. But apparently, her group is done with their short film, and I'm trying not to let that panic me.

The hotel lobby has been cleared where we're filming. Josh has got the camera on Jace—we already got Audrey's side—and he yawns, shaking his head after to keep himself awake.

"We should run that one more time," I say after Jace finishes his line.

"Seriously, again?" Jace growls from his marker. He crouches in place, huffing at the floor. We only have a couple of days of shooting in the hotel, and I'm a genius who picked mostly night shoots, so we're all running on Red Bull and anger.

"I'm just… not feeling it." It's not them. Jace has chemistry with everyone, including Audrey.

It's my writing. It's the words on the page they're trying to act, but it's not working. Not genuine. Forced.

And too soon.

How do I write a proclamation of love when the characters have only known each other for a few days? I studied. I watched How to Lose a Guy in Ten Days *twice*, because technically, I was a little distracted because Liz was with me.

I made out during a movie. She's corrupted me.

I scratch at my hat, tipping it slightly from my ear.

Jace sighs again, his eyes flicking toward the front door as a couple rolls in their luggage. "We have the place tomorrow night, too, yeah?"

"Yeah…" But I was hoping to get everything done tonight. Get through the dailies, go to work, then spend tomorrow night with Liz.

"Let's call it, then." Jace looks at Audrey for support, and she gladly gives it to him. The circles under her eyes are getting darker, and that's probably not best for filming, anyway.

"'Kay," I relent. "Tomorrow at five, then."

"Bring food next time." Jace stretches his arms to the ceiling, a resounding crack from his neck echoing around us. "I don't work for free."

If I had the energy, I'd kick his ass. Instead, I settle for the bird and pull out my phone. Five missed calls, five new voicemails.

And they aren't from Liz.

Our group packs up while I try to ignore the sudden weight my phone has to it. My mom never calls only once, and I have to mentally prepare myself for whatever she's grousing about today.

It takes us a good half hour to get things torn down and into my car, but even that isn't enough time. I doubt a year would be enough. I grip my steering wheel, waiting till my knuckles turn white. Then I bite the bullet and return her calls.

It rings once before her voice comes through.

"You drunk or something?" she answers, no how-do-you-dos. The TV plays loudly in the background. "Out partying?"

"Hey, Ma."

"I saw Rosie today. I told her you'd give her a call."

My jaw clicks. Mom only tries to set me up with someone when I'm with someone else. Just her way of telling me I don't know how to pick them.

"I'm seeing someone," I remind her. Not like it matters.

"She'll be home this summer." The background noise silences, except for my father's booming voice complaining that she paused the TV. "You two can catch up. Get together."

"*I* won't be home this summer." We've been over it a thousand times. Mom only lets what she wants to hear sink in, though. "If I get the grant, I'll start filming."

"Thought you had that girlfriend." *Now* she acknowledges Liz's existence. "Didn't think you had time to work on that... movie."

The way she says the word grates on my every last nerve. It's been almost five years since I left PA, nothing but a camera, computer, and a hundred bucks to my name. And she still expects me to drop it all, run home with my tail between my legs, and marry whoever she deems worthy.

I'm keeping Liz far away from her for as long as I possibly can.

"I just left a shoot." I rub my eyes, too tired for this. I knew I should've waited to call back. Or not call back at all. But the day I don't I know it'll be an actual emergency. "Lizzie isn't a distraction."

That's a bold-faced lie. She's the ultimate distraction, but I'm still trying to convince myself she's also my inspiration.

"I sent you Rosie's number," Mom says, like the last minute of conversation didn't happen. The TV turns on, and the relief that she'll hang up soon washes over me. "Let me know how it goes."

The line drops, and I let my phone clatter into the cupholder. It's late, and I told Liz I had to focus tonight. But all I want is her in my arms, her raspberry scent clinging onto my sheets, and her body curled against mine.

My car heads to her place. My feet climb her steps. My mouth tells her I want her tonight. My hands help her pack an overnight bag. Then they squeeze her hand twice.

She's all smiles and hugs and everything that is so foreign to me, but I like it. I crave it. I want it more than I've wanted anything. The only thing I've ever wanted this badly was a career in film, directing, living in LA… But I don't want it alone.

And that scares me more than anything.

TWELVE

LIAM: I love you. It's been three days, and I know absolutely nothing about love. I know I've never felt it. I've felt the obligatory kind of love—the kind I have for my family. My mom, dad, sister… yeah, I love them. But I don't like them most days, and so that makes it weird to say I love them, because I don't think that's how love is supposed to feel.

Liam pauses, gathering his growing thoughts, ~~scratching at his hat~~. Layla blinks, mouth slightly parted. Her hand doesn't leave his.

LIAM: I love my friends, but that's more like what family love is supposed to be, I think. They are like family, or what my family would be if I got to choose them. I like them and love them, but I'm not going to share my life with them, and that's okay. So, that's not close to what I'm feeling either.

Liam starts to play with Layla's fingers, tapping them knuckle to knuckle. Layla watches the movements, quiet, confused, patient.

LIAM: You are walking sunshine, ~~Lizzie~~. You are kindness and warmth and passion, and I want every moment with you, even when I know it's not good for what I've planned for myself. Even if I don't know how long it will last.

I've never felt this way, so... it has to be love. I've never felt love, but I think... this is how it feels. I hope this is how it feels. It's intense and beautiful, and I hope to God you feel even just a pinch of it.

A knock comes at my door, and I slam the laptop shut, my confession only halfway out of my head and onto the page. Alec pushes off the couch to answer, but Liz cracks it open, and he sits back down.

"Should've figured." He chuckles and settles his headphones on, pulling his computer onto his lap. Liz gives him a wave, her duffel hitting the floor with a plop.

"How was the shoot?" She slinks onto my lap, her bright green eyes genuinely curious about how my project is going. Even though it's not-going.

I give her hand two pumps. She pumps once back. "I still can't get this scene right."

"What scene?"

"The declaration." When she lifts a brow, I elaborate. "It's the plot point in Act Three when one or both of the protagonists declares their intentions or feelings for each other."

"Hmm." She tucks one of the couch pillows against her chest. "Who's telling who?"

"He's telling her."

"Maybe switch it up." Her nail runs over the stitching along the side of the pillow. "She's been the bold one, right? He's all shy and cute—even though Jace is *not* that."

We share a laugh, and by the way Alec's shoulders bounce, I take it his headphones aren't completely blocking out our conversation.

"Thought it might be good for his character development." I follow the patterns she's tracing on the pillow, if only to touch her in another place we aren't currently touching.

"Not yet, right?" She bops my knuckle. "They haven't had their dark moment. So maybe she confesses, and he doesn't, and that's what causes things to be left a little…" Her brows pull inward, and I try to help out.

"Underwhelming?"

"No… that's not the word."

"Devastating."

"Not that harsh." She laughs, linking our hands. "It's like, not as exciting… oh my gosh, why can't I think of the wor—?"

"Anti-climatic," Alec says, not taking his eyes off his screen.

Liz bounces on my lap. "Yes. That one."

I tilt my head. "Don't I want a climactic moment for my climax?"

"The I love you isn't the climax, is it?"

"Kinda…"

"Then what's their dark moment?"

I grind my teeth. I've avoided a dark moment. I hate them. In Ever After, shit hit the fan when he found out who she really was. In Never Been Kissed, shit hit the fan when he found out who she really was. In She's the Man, shit hit the fan when he found out who she really was.

Liz continues to play with my hand, running her fingers up and down every knuckle. I hope I already know who she is, but given the history of rom com, I don't know at all.

"I… Well, I don't want to give them one."

"Every relationship has a dark moment, Landon."

"I refuse to accept that."

"Find a rom com without one." She reaches for my hat, and I let her. "It's part of the formula."

"The formula sucks."

She faux gasps, bringing her hand to her chest after settling my hat on her head. "You take that back! Dark moments are pivotal!"

"Explain that to me."

"Without them, the relationship is too perfect."

"What's wrong with perfection?" I'm certainly finding nothing wrong with it. Other than the fact that I can't get any damn work done.

"It's not *real*."

"Movies aren't real."

"The emotions they evoke are. And trust me, every girl wants a guy to want them when they are not perfect."

"I want you," I counter, my mouth spewing off before

I can stop it.

She lets out a large snort. "Exactly. I am not perfect."

"I beg to differ."

"Landon, so help me, I will fart on your lap right now to prove a point."

Alec shuts his laptop then, silently taking it to his room. Liz and I share a laugh, and I start tickling her, she tickles back, and then we're kissing and moving to my bedroom. My short film is a distant memory—as well as every other thought in my head—as she proves just how perfect she is for me.

***

Liz adjusts on the bed, sitting up and scrolling through her phone, allowing me to watch mindlessly over her shoulder. Her hair is half out of her ponytail, half still tucked in from our roll-around. I love that she leaves it that way, that she feels no need to "fix" herself. I reach over and squeeze her thigh twice.

The corner of her mouth twitches upward. "You do that a lot."

"What?"

She puts her phone on the nightstand, sliding in next to me. Goosebumps rush up my leg when her cold feet tap my skin.

"You always squeeze my hand twice."

I swallow hard, tempted to squeeze her twice against me. It's become such a habit. "Yeah."

She doesn't press me, and pretty soon, her breathing

levels out. She flips to her side, facing the window, allowing me more room, even though I don't want it.

I should've known she'd pick up on it. Liz is smart, among many other things, and she doesn't hold back from saying how she feels or what she's thinking. Unlike me.

I sure as hell thought I didn't know how to say I love her… but, well, I have been saying it.

And she's caught on.

The word that's been pasted onto my tongue, threatening to have a voice, wakes up with a bite. I roll over, leaning up on my arm. Her hair is still a mess, an indent from her watch imprinted on her cheek.

"Tumbles?" I whisper into the dark. She doesn't move a muscle. And that somehow makes my smile even wider, my nerves double in intensity.

I press my lips to her cheek. She twitches, rolling slightly, so she's on her back. I run my hand over her stomach, tracing patterns over her warm skin.

"Tumbles…" I sing it this time. I'm tone deaf, and I don't care. She stirs, letting out a whiny groan. As soon as her eyes flutter open and lock with mine, I take her face into my hands. "Two squeezes mean I love you."

Her lips part, and she blinks. Once. Twice. Three times. I drop a palm from her cheek and find hers resting near her hip. My heart thumps clean from my chest and settles against hers.

I squeeze her hand twice.

"I've been too afraid to say it." Heat creeps up my

neck. "But I've been saying it to you for a long time now."

Her eyes flip back and forth between mine, sleepiness and shock melting away as she takes in my admission.

Her lips curve upward, and she squeezes my hand once. "I've been saying I love you too for a long time now."

I meet her smile, covering her mouth with mine. She wraps her arms around my neck, squeezes twice, and I squeeze back, and we silently say I love you over and over.

No dark moment needed.

#4: OCTOBER SKY

1999

DIRECTED BY JOE JOHNSTON

I'll admit... this one is on my list because it parallels my life a little too accurately. From the moment Homer saw Sputnik in the sky, he fell in love with rocketry. He studied it, dedicated his every waking moment to building and learning. He didn't worry about befriending the outcast or failing a few hundred times. The teasing from his older brother, the lack of support from his father... It didn't matter. He persevered.

From the moment I watched my first movie, I knew something was magical about them. Homer wanted to focus on the sky instead of what was in the ground, something that was all his town was known for.

I wanted out of reality. I wanted to focus on the stories, the fantasies, the entertainment.

I watched October Sky in my first film studies class. I watched it again later that week, and another time that same month, and then multiple times when I caught it on TV. I've seen it more times than I can count.

And every time, I can't shut down the ache from the apathy of his family... or the joy of seeing Homer's dream come true.

Thirteen

"It's not bad," Professor Driver says, stopping the footage he asked to review. Jace shifts out of the corner of my eye, but I'm too laser focused to see what sort of expression he's wearing.

"Any notes?" I prod. Professor Driver's pen flew across his notebook while he watched, and with every mark of ink, the knot in my gut got more and more impossible to unravel.

It's shit. I know it. Jace knows it. By the looks on Josh and Audrey's faces, they know it, too. And it's April, and we're approaching that deadline way too quickly, and I'm out of hotel shoots, and I don't know how the hell I'll get an airport shoot done, and my knee keeps bouncing, sweat forming underneath my hat, and I bet Professor Driver is ready to stomp all over my dreams and tell me to prepare for life in that call center that is slowly killing me.

"It's not as complete as it should be," he starts, jotting down another thing in that notebook. "Your five acts are a little… undefined."

Don't have to tell me. "Which ones in particular?" I

take out my own notebook, ready to pull in any advice he has and put it into practice.

"All of them." He lets out a laugh to ease the blow, but it doesn't.

Jace shifts again, leaning forward enough to get more in my periphery. "Well, shit."

"I'm not saying it's that," Professor Driver muses, steepling his fingers. "It's unfocused. Let's look at the five act structure and tear it down a bit. I'm just going to ask questions. No need to answer them here… answer them here." He points to the computer screen paused on the last shot I had filmed and edited.

I take a deep breath and poise my pen. For the next half hour, I frantically jot down every word he says, not knowing a damn answer to anything. Why is it so important for Liam to return to his hometown? What's holding him back from committing to Layla? Why is Layla so perfect? Where are her flaws? What is her qualms about falling in love?

All great questions. All have the same answer.

Because I know absolute shit about romance. Despite all the studying. Despite falling in actual love. There is a block in the brain and over my heart, and I don't know how to break it down.

I manage to take it all in stride. Even Jace feels the blow; he lets out the biggest exhale when we step out of Professor Driver's office, along with a slew of profanity.

"Do we have time to do all this?"

"Rewrite and reshoot everything?" A defeated snort rumbles my nose and sort of hurts my throat. "No."

"I don't think we have to start from scratch," Audrey says.. "I agree we need to figure out more about Liam and Layla. Maybe let me take a stab at the script? Or I can sit down with you."

Her face is hopeful, and a string of panic gets plucked in my gut, reverberating through my body. I don't know if I want the help. I don't want to admit I might need it.

"What's your schedule like?" she offers when I don't answer. I pull my phone out and bring up my calendar.

"I guess I have some time next Wednesday before class."

"Perfect. We can meet then. Will you send me the doc?"

I swallow around the lump in my throat. "Sure."

The rest of the plans muffle in my ears. I don't want to see the scribbles all up and down this damn script. I have to send her parts at a time, when I've gone through it and taken out the more personal stuff. I've gotten too caught up in the real-life romance that the script is suffering from it.

Real romance isn't movie romance.

"Let's meet up this weekend," Josh says. "We can reshoot some of the elevator scenes at our building."

I slightly nod. We've used their apartment building for some of the interior elevator shots. Guess that's all we can do for now. Audrey and Josh take off in one direction, Jace and I in the other as we make our way through campus.

"Man, I'm sorry," Jace says after a few minutes.

"For what?" It's not his fault the thing is crap. There were no notes on the acting. Jace and Audrey are doing the best with the shit I've given them to work with.

"Feels like I haven't done anything to help out." He scratches at his face; the beard I asked him to grow for the character is getting a little too long. "I just let you tell me what to do."

"In all fairness, that's how I prefer it." My script, my vision, his execution, my editing. Not the winning formula I thought it would be.

"We should take the night off," he says after another beat.

"Funny."

"I'm serious." He cracks his knuckles. "Get a drink, go out… no *movies*."

I shake my head. If I'm letting Audrey anywhere near the script, I have to rewrite a shit ton of it. "We don't have time."

"It's an important part of the creative process." He mocks. "Gotta let Professor Driver's notes percolate before acting on them."

Oh, they're percolating all right. Festering in my brain and infecting my confidence.

I set my jaw. "Sorry. Going to work on it."

Jace growls and pulls his phone out.

"You aren't seeing what clubs are open, are you?"

"No, you dead weight." His fingers fly across his

screen. "I'm texting Lizzie."

I jolt. I don't want Liz to know about all this. "Why?"

"So she can distract you."

"Please don't."

"Too late." He grins as he shows the message that's already sent. Her three bouncing dots pop up in the thread.

My jaw clicks, and I ignore his attempts at getting me in a better mood. Jace doesn't give two shits about the grant, so what's this to him? He doesn't have a script on his laptop waiting for funding. He doesn't work at a job that kills him just to keep him from moving back home with his tail between his legs.

Her message pops up. *Tell him to swing by and get me! I'm more than happy to help him out tonight* 😊

The thought of watching movie after movie, Googling and watching documentaries and interviews hollows my gut. I can't involve Liz. She's not the inspiration I thought she'd be. She's too perfect, and like she said... movies need imperfection.

The way she smiles, laughs, grimaces, teases... How her southern accent comes out when she's babbling. When she dances after biting into dessert. Her haphazard ponytails she never fixes after we've made love. The way she sleeps on me like she's a backpack. Her snorts and fart threats and chipped nail polish... I can't find a flaw in any of that.

The only flaw I can even think of when it comes to her is... she's muddied the waters of what I want in life. It used to be a clear river, leading straight to Hollywood. I could hop in my boat and take off, knowing exactly where I was going and how I was getting there.

I've never been a realist, but it's happening. My feet are coming down to earth, and instead of Hollywood, life with a wife, kids, working a 9-5 are somewhere in the distance. It's murky and blurred, and I don't know what that's going to look like for me, and I have no clue how to get there. No plan. Other than I'm pretty sure Liz is next to me, holding my hand, squeezing it twice.

FOURTEEN

"You're so sad." Lizzie pokes at my lips, squishing them together so they can't frown. I bite at her, but it's half-hearted, since my heart is so damn tired.

She shifts, her hip bumping mine on the couch before she gets on her knees. Her hair is down, swooping over her shoulders and tickling my forearm. "Can I watch it?" she asks, nerves trembling her bottom lip.

I lift the bill of my cap to get a better look at her. "The short film?"

She nods. "Maybe I can offer some insight."

My stomach hollows. "I'll tell you right now what that insight would be." I wave at the pile of notes sitting on the opposite side of the couch. "Shit. All shit. I need to give up."

"Over one opinion?" She crosses her arms. "What are you going to do when Rodgers gives you a thumbs up and Eberts gives you a thumbs down?"

A laugh barrels from deep in my hollowed gut, and I pull her to me. "That is the same man, Tumbles."

She tilts her head, her knees settling on either side of

my hips. "No… It's those two critics who used to do that show."

"Roger Ebert and Gene Siskel."

"Rogers and Eberts."

I laugh again, rocking her in my lap. "And you got into an advanced theater course how?"

She pinches my lips shut. "Quiet you. My point is, you can't give up over one opinion." Her fingers drop from my face, but I take them in my hand. I can't seem to go a minute in her presence without touching some part of her, and that's on a good day. Bad days? Well, I don't want to admit just how much I need this hand holding.

"It was a pretty important opinion, Lizzie."

"And mine isn't?" She jabs her pointer into my sternum. "I am the woman you love, damn it."

"This is true." I lean in to kiss her, but she gives me the cheek. "Really?"

"No lip for you until you show me."

"I can kiss other places." I prove my point by attacking the spot she likes on her neck. She giggles and squirms and screams out, "Cheater!" and I don't give a shit if I get the grant in the ten seconds I have her in my arms.

She wriggles from my grasp, tripping over the pillows we'd thrown on the floor to get across the room.

"Stay," she says, like I'm a dog in training. She eases toward my laptop. Her eyes don't leave mine, and they are playful, yet serious, and I wonder how I could direct Audrey to give that same look in one of the scenes we're reshooting this weekend.

Liz sits at the table, lifting the laptop lid. Something a lot like nerves and stomach acid build on the back of my tongue.

"Don't." It comes out much sharper than I intended. I gulp and add, "Please."

She tilts her head. She wants to be playful. She thinks *I'm* being playful. That's what we do, who we are.

But a ripple of irritation runs up the back of my neck as her finger hovers over the mousepad.

"Liz…"

"Really?" Her hand drops to the side of the laptop. "I can't watch it?"

"No." It's a piece of shit, and I don't want her to see that. I don't want her to see how incompetent I am. I don't want advice from her, or a pitying review. I don't want to realize the dream I've worked for is dead because I can't direct a damn kissing scene. Or what if that isn't even the issue? What if it's everything, not just the genre? If I handed Professor Driver the zombie script, would the notes be the same? The film isn't missing something—*I'm* missing something.

The tease in her eyes fades, relaxing the smile I see so often. "How can I help?"

She can't. I don't want her to. "I'm fine."

Her brow lifts, and we both know I'm lying through my teeth. "Have you thought about handing the reins to Jace for a bit?"

I let out a humorless laugh. "He's not the most reliable partner."

"Is it that?" She crosses her arms, swiveling slightly to face me. "Or you won't *let* him?"

That irritation crawling up my neck burns my ears, turning quickly into annoyance. "What are you getting at?"

"You can't really complain about doing everything yourself if you don't take help when it's offered."

"I don't want you to watch it," I snap. She jerks from my tone—one I've never used around her. I'm shocked I'm still capable of it, to be honest. I haven't used it since I left Philadelphia. Growing up in a state of constant defense was exhausting. I promised myself I wasn't going to make an argument out of everything.

I pull my hat off and toss it on the cushion next to me, forcing a deep breath to relax my shoulders and soften my voice. "I don't need another person telling me what I'm doing wrong."

"You assume I'm going to tear it to shreds?"

"I'm sure you'll sugarcoat it. But I don't want to be patronized, either."

Her lips purse, and the air turns ice cold between us. "I have a brain, you know. Just because I'm a little ditsy doesn't mean I won't have good suggestions."

What the hell? "I didn't call you ditsy." I'd never think it either.

"You just made fun of me for not knowing about Roger Eberts or whatever."

"I was teasing." How in the world did this conversation get here? "Liz, it's *because* I value your opinion that I don't want it."

"That makes no sense." She twists in her seat, and I itch to go to her. It's an itch I have to scratch, and I rise from the couch. Her eyes watch my every step, a watery wall building that wrings my heart.

I crouch next to her, using some effort to get her hand from her tightly crossed arms. "I can't mess this up. If I don't get the grant, I'll be working at that damn call center for at least another five years, overtime, double overtime, just to get enough to fund the project sitting on my laptop. And in five years, that project will be past its time. Trends move so fast, and I need to hop on it."

Her jaw relaxes, and she leans in, kissing my knuckles. "I get that. I want it *for* you."

"I know." It's one of the many reasons I love her.

"Then explain why I can't watch it. Why I can't help you. Because it feels like you're hiding something or that you don't trust me, and it's not a great feeling, Landon."

The corner of my mouth twitches. Even frustration looks good on her. "I love you, Tumbles."

"Yes."

"And if I let you watch it—"

"You'd be the best boyfriend ever."

"And you don't like it—"

"I will."

"I might not recover."

Her eyes widen, and she squeezes my hand twice. I squeeze back. "Why are you so hard on yourself, Landon?"

I shake my head. "It's bad. I need you to trust me on that."

"Then let. Me. Help." She scrunches her lips together. "Damn it, you are making me angry."

"You are very cute angry."

"Dangerous words, mister." She nudges my chest, and I rock on my heels. "If I can't watch it, then how can I help?"

She still doesn't get it. I don't want her in my head, in my work. I don't want a person sitting there to disappoint. I've disappointed my family my whole life by just existing.

"I work better alone."

"How do you know?" she asks with a cocky tilt of her head. "Have you *tried* to work with someone?"

An exasperated breath leaves my nostrils, a deep growl building in the back of my throat. "Liz, I'm serious. I don't want your help. I need to figure this out alone. No distractions, no notes… Can we drop it?"

The ice cold air returns, and she straightens in her seat, sliding her hand from mine. "Okay."

It sounds anything but okay. She pushes from her seat, nearly knocking me to my ass. Her jacket is in her hand in the next second.

"Where are you going?"

"You work better alone." She won't meet my eyes, but her voice is sticky and wet. "So I'll leave you to it."

"You don't have to leave."

"I think I do." She waves her hair out from her jacket, the raspberry scent that clings onto every strand filling the air. "I'll be back when the project is done."

She smiles—a very different one than I've seen—and kisses me on the cheek. I reach for her, but she's too fast, leaving me grasping air. My feet won't lift from the floor, and I watch like an idiot as she walks out.

#3: THE PURSUIT OF HAPPYNESS

2006

DIRECTED BY GABRIELE MUCCINO

My mother taught me how to solve a Rubik's cube when I was eighteen, right before graduation.

We were all in the living room, surprisingly, as a family. Dad was in his recliner. Mom was in her robe, folding socks from the laundry basket. Elle was flipping her attention between her book and the TV.

The Pursuit of Happyness was on. I'd seen it—went when it was in theaters and cried in front of half a dozen buddies. Dad was channel surfing when he stopped on the scene with Will Smith ogling a Ferrari. Being a car guy, I wasn't surprised he paused.

"You seen this?" he asked me from his chair. I was scribbling in my notebook, butt going numb against the worn carpet.

"Yep."

"It any good?"

"Yep."

If I raved about it, I knew he'd turn the channel. Being my predictable father, he set the remote down and got sucked in.

Mom was sucked in.

Elle was sucked in.

And for two hours, we were a family who seemed to have something in common. Could've been the fact that we've never been well-off. Not poverty, by any means, but lower class. Mom didn't work. Dad was a tow truck driver. Our house sat in not the best of neighborhoods.

So with the entire plot revolving around working hard and hoping to God it pays off, guess they were all waiting to see if that really would happen.

"I can do that," Mom said when Will Smith solved the Rubik's cube in the back of a cab.

My pencil stopped in the middle of my sentence, and I swiveled to look at my mother. "The Rubik's cube?"

"Mmhmm."

She said it like she'd actively told us things like this about herself all our lives. Her cavalier attitude had every one of us staring. Dad even paused the TV.

"You can not."

"Bet me." She tossed a pair of socks into the basket. "Get one in my hands, and I'll prove you all wrong."

We didn't own a Rubik's cube, but the Walmart down the street was only charging four bucks for one. Since I'd seen the movie, I was tasked to get it. Curiosity carried my feet faster through the aisles. I wanted to see her do it. I wanted to see us all enraptured by her.

When I crossed the threshold, Dad, Mom, and Elle... all of them... Tears down their cheeks. Dad swiped them so fast I didn't catch the actual tears, just the redness in his eyes. Mom was glued to the screen, her jaw tight, a single tear dropping from her chin. Elle was sobbing, her chin on her knees, her book forgotten on the arm of the couch.

I heard what scene it was before I saw it. The

pounding against the bathroom door, the swell of the music.

And I smiled.

That scene is damn heartbreaking, even more so when I found out it was factual. And it had hit the heart of my heartless family.

And this movie I had tossed aside as just another on the pile became one of my favorites.

FIFTEEN

I am useless.

My face falls onto my keyboard, adding who knows what to the ending of this script. Audrey has texted me at least five times, asking for the document. I've been a stubborn jackass, refusing to send it in its current state.

It's been two days since I've seen Liz. Two. That's it. And it feels like it's been years.

I miss her hand. I miss squeezing it. I miss having her in my bed. I miss my bed period. It was three in the morning last I checked, and when I lift my head, it's only 3:02. Time is moving like frozen honey, and I should appreciate it, since I have a dozen reshoots planned.

My phone sits idle by my left hand, and my fingers twitch. I could text her. I could stop being so damn stubborn and let her watch this piece of shit I call a movie. But I want to fix so much before I do. The first kiss needs some work. I can't decide whether to go with funny or romantic on that one. Not to mention the fact it's practically a play-by-play reenactment of our first kiss. Would she laugh? Cringe? Remember I have zero game and lucked the hell out actually getting her to fall in love with me?

A low growl erupts from my twisted stomach, and I bang my head on the keyboard. I can't do this without her, but what the hell did I do before? I've written several scripts. I've won awards, damn it. So what is this non-functioning shit?

I eye the pile of DVDs next to my Xbox, the pinks, purples, and reds all splashed on every cover. I could've counted on my hand how many romantic comedies I voluntarily watched before this semester. Mom and Elle were never ones to pop them in, and Dad sure as hell wasn't going to. Film classes required a few, and I honestly thought they were showing the best of the best, so I figured I didn't need them, especially since I wanted to venture more into comedy without the romance.

Romance in movies wasn't real life. It wasn't hand holding or thinking about that person every second or blundering through first dates. Romance to me was more or less tolerance of another person long enough to get married, have kids, and… Well, that was all I had to go on.

My hand twitches again. It's three in the morning; no way she's awake. But I want to call her, anyway. Wake her up. Ask her a million questions. My heart does a hard beat against my chest, constricting my airway for half a second. I'm going to get chewed out, but I curl my hand around my phone and risk it.

I don't have to scroll too far to get to her name. She called me six times yesterday while I was at work and another three when I was shooting. I ignore the shake in my thumb as I hit the call button and the hitch in my breath when I put the phone to my ear.

It rings only once before her voice cuts through the pounding of my heart. "Are you drunk?"

I swallow hard. "Hi, Ma."

She coughs. A baritone voice grumbles in the background, and she says, "It's your son."

"Sorry it's so late."

"I was up. Your dad keeps turning on his left side."

"Gotcha." That's his "snoring" side, and anyone who has lived within a five-mile radius of their house knows just how loud that side can get. "Well, I… I had a question for you."

"You still haven't answered mine. You drunk?"

"No."

"You sure?"

"Yes."

"Is that Lily or whoever making you drink?"

"Liz. And I'm not drunk." I am questioning my brain function, though. "I'm working on my movie—"

"Still?" She yawns. "You always were a procrastinator."

My jaw clicks. I'm the farthest thing from a procrastinator. "I've been working on it all semester, Ma."

"It only has to be fifteen minutes. You'd be done by now."

"A lot of work goes into fifteen minutes of footage."

Especially if I'm unfamiliar with the genre, got writer's block, the pressure to win the grant, and working a full-time job and going to school. She knows all this, but that doesn't matter.

I blow out a breath. I'm not going to argue with her over stupid things. She's always right, even when she's dead wrong.

"You love Dad, right?"

The longest pause—for my mother—follows. I figured I'd get the reason for my call out there before I hang up out of frustration.

She lets out a single *ha* that I think is a laugh, but I haven't heard one from her in a long time. "What did you drink, Landon? Whiskey? Scotch? Tequila? I don't think you can handle it."

I bite my tongue. She can think I'm drunk; I don't give a shit anymore. "How did you fall in love with him?"

The second longest pause follows that question, and I take the opportunity to grab my notebook. There has to be love that started their relationship. More than tolerance, more than obligation. They made the choice to get married, to *stay* married, to have a family.

"Jesus, Landon. I don't know. It's been thirty years."

"You don't remember how you fell in love?" I'm holding out hope, and not just because I'm stuck on this movie. If I'm lucky enough to get thirty years with Lizzie, I want to remember how I fell in love with her. How it slapped me across the face. How I didn't know what the hell it was, because I'd never felt it before. I want to double-squeeze that hand when we're thirty, forty, fifty… ninety.

I don't want to forget. I don't want any of our kids to question if I love her or not. It will be incredibly obvious.

I'm planning an entire future with this woman I've known for less than a year. And my mother can't tell me any of her past with the man she's loved for over thirty.

My shoulders slump, and I drop the pen, letting it roll into the crease of the notebook. I don't know what the hell possessed me to call, or what made me think it'd be a productive conversation. "Forget it—"

"Mouse Trap."

My spine straightens. "Huh?"

Mom lets out a deep breath that ends in a soft chuckle. "Your dad gave me Mouse Trap."

I have the urge to ask her if she's drunk. "The board game?"

"Yep." Her voice turns airy, and it hits me like the THX logo, waking me up in an instant. "I wanted so badly to play it as a kid. Your uncles Brian and Richard would play on our kitchen table and refused to let me join. They would always say I had to be eight years old, because 'that's what it said on the box.'"

Her imitation of her brothers gets a laugh out of me. I lean against the back of my chair, running a hand along my hairline. "Elle did that to me a few times."

"I'm not surprised." She chuckles again, and that's three times she's laughed in this conversation, which is more than I can count for the entire year. "So, when I turned eight, I was so excited. It was the one thing I waited for on my birthday. I woke the whole house yelling, 'Today is the day I play Mouse Trap!' I should've known something was up with Brian and Richard were all too excited to watch me pull it from the shelf."

"Did they break it?"

"You could say that," she says humorlessly. "They would say otherwise."

"What'd they do?"

"They super-glued all the traps. Every piece."

I'm not too familiar with the game, but I take it gluing doesn't make it very fun. An ache of sorrow pangs my chest, surprising me. I've never felt much sympathy for any members of my family. Sympathy wasn't exactly a thing at our house. Or any other emotion besides annoyance.

"Did they get the belt?" I try to joke. Grandma and Grandpa were known for laying down the hammer.

She lets out a growl mixed with a snort I'm unsure how to interpret. "Oh no. They all thought it was hilarious. Prank of the year! Mouse Trap was proudly displayed in the living room hutch for years."

"I remember that hutch." Vaguely. There are only flashes of it, foggy and blurred. There was a clock in there with a terrifying frog sitting on top of what was supposed to be a lily pad but looked more like a head of lettuce. Never saw Mouse Trap.

"It was in there when your dad took me to prom. He'd

asked me because we had mutual friends who were going. Grandma told him all about the game when he asked why we had it in the hutch next to other porcelain trinkets. It did look out of place."

"So he bought it for you?" Dad has always been prone to giving things instead of actually expressing himself. He bought me my first video camera after I hung a poster on the wall and told him I was going to be a director.

"Oh, a few months later. I didn't even think he remembered. It was such a small conversation. Less than a minute, I'd say." Nostalgia hits her tone, almost blissful. I honestly didn't think my mother was capable of a thing. "It was my eighteenth birthday. He asked me out—we'd only been out a few times since prom, here and there over the summer. He didn't want to get too serious with me, I don't think, since he was a few years older, and I was still in high school."

"So you finally got to play the game?"

She laughs. "No. He gave me the one that was in the hutch."

I sit straight up. "What?" Here I thought this was a romantic story. Should've known.

"He stole it right from my mother's house, wrapped it up, and then handed me a hammer."

A chuckle works its way across my tongue. "Wait… that's when you fell in love?"

"He could've gotten down on one knee right there, and I would've said yes."

I shake my head. Clearly, I know nothing. "Why?"

"A million other men would've bought a new game for me. But he took that same one and let me destroy it, so I didn't have to look at the thing or relive the story any time someone asked about it. And they asked a lot."

A new respect for my dad and his intuition flows through me. "Didn't realize Dad had such game."

"He doesn't." And just as she says it, a loud snore filters through the background, and we both laugh.

"I'd say I should let you get back to sleep, but…"

"My chair is comfortable," she says.

"Is that far enough away?" I joke.

"Once I roll him over." She yawns. "Oh! Before I forget, Rosie said you never called her."

My shoulders deflate. "Ma, we just had a good conversation. Can we not ruin it?"

"I just talked about love. Rosie is a good segue."

"I have Lizzie—"

"Send her a message. That's all I'm saying."

I sigh. "Goodnight, Ma."

"Sober up, son." She clicks off, and I set the phone down, unsure if I'm more or less confused than I was before I called.

#2: LITTLE MISS SUNSHINE

2006

DIRECTED BY JONATHAN DAYTON AND VALERIE FARIS (DEBUT DIRECTORS!)

Sundance.

First year there.

Best year ever.

The top prize for the first film contest I ever entered—tickets to Sundance.

And I got it.

I had a plus one, and Alec was it. No one complained. Dad doesn't like to fly. Mom says Utah is a place religious people judge you all day. Elle said it would be a nightmare spending a week with only me for company.

It's ironic that the movie I got to see was all about a strained family growing together, travelling across the country just for one member's dream.

It was a fantasy—one I wanted. One I've wished for.

MASTER OF THE MEET CUTE

Critics praised it for being so real. But hell, I praise it for being something to strive for.

I might not get that with my own family—the closeness, the understanding, the do everything and anything for each other. But I damn sure will do that for the family I create.

SIXTEEN

My laptop bag strap slips from my shoulder, and I hoist it up. I tap my thigh to an unknown beat, breathing harder than I should for just standing outside Lizzie's door.

Maybe I'll blame the three flights I just climbed.

The deadbolt clicks on the other side of the door, the chain lock rattling. Liz opens it wide enough for only her, a hand on her hip.

"Hey."

I swallow hard. She's damn gorgeous, even when she's pissed at me. Her pajama bottoms have little coffee cups on them, her tank top hanging loose and low, the words *I need a Latte sleep* splayed across her chest. Her lips are pressed together, so I can't see the gap that drives me nuts.

She painted her nails. Silver. Her right thumb is chipping.

I adjust my bag and take a deep breath, pushing the word I hate out of my throat. "Help me?"

Her hand falls from her hip. The tough edge to her eyes softens. Her lips part slightly.

There's that gap.

"I need your help, Tumbles." The word is easier the second time. "Will you watch it? Tell me what you think?"

A hint of a smile touches the corners of her mouth. "Of course." She opens the door for me.

But I step into her instead. My thumb touches her chin. "My lips miss yours."

She bites back a smile. "They can say hello."

I mean to kiss her softly, but the time apart urges for harder, more passionate. She meets my intensity, her fingers hooking my belt loops and bringing us chest to chest. Her tongue taps a question against my lips, and I don't hesitate to answer.

Never again, my brain whispers. *Three days apart was too long.*

She tugs me inside, our lips still attached to each other. I kick the door shut, holding her in my hands, never wanting to let her go again. Thank Christ this fight wasn't the end of things. I honestly wasn't sure. My track record with relationships isn't great, and communicating isn't my strong suit, either. But damn it, I will learn. For her. For us.

Her palm slithers up my chest, and the slightest nudge from her, and I back up.

She whoopie cushions. I love her random raspberries. I press a kiss to her nose, the apples of her cheeks, her chin, move down her neck. She groans, rumbling the tip of my nose.

"If you really want my help, you have to stop."

I do. But I keep kissing her anyway. She giggles a

frustrated giggle, which is growled and high-pitched and so damn adorable.

I've missed more than her lips, that's for sure.

"Landon," she scolds. My mouth pauses over her left breast, knowing if I kiss there, I will feel her heartbeat, want to take her to the bedroom, forget the entire reason I'm here.

I blow out a breath and reluctantly let her go, dropping my arms from around her waist. She catches my hand before I can get too far.

Squeezes it twice.

I squeeze once.

"Anything I should know before I start it?" she asks, pulling the strap from my shoulder. Her neck is flushed, distracting me for a split second.

I run my hand over the back of my head, knocking my hat off center. "It's a piece of shit."

She rolls her eyes, taking the laptop from its sleeve. "You are in desperate need of another opinion, then."

Her hips shake, the skin between her tank and pajama pants teasing me as she plops on her couch, settling the laptop in her lap. Nerves simmer in my gut, leaving an acrid taste on the back of my tongue.

"Don't say I didn't warn you," I mumble. She waves me off, then pats the spot next to her.

My nerves turn to a boil, and I shake my head.

"You're not going to watch with me?" She frowns.

"I don't think I can watch you watch it," I admit. "I'll

analyze every facial expression, every twitch, every gasp or lack of laughter at a joke, and I don't want to put all that pressure on you as a watcher—"

"I'm hungry."

I jerk at her change of pace. "You're always hungry."

"Yep." She pulls her legs up, sitting crisscross applesauce. "I could do Chinese, pizza, tacos…"

Her hint clicks into my brain. My keys are in my hand within the next second, and I give her a kiss on the forehead.

"Back in an hour."

***

The film is only ten minutes, and that's because it's an incomplete piece of garbage. But I take my time getting the food, anyway.

The worst possible scenarios run through my head. She'll hate it so much that she'll dump me. Or maybe she'll be offended by some of the scenes because they are a little too close to things we have done or said to each other. Or maybe she doesn't find it funny at all. She realizes I'm a fraud. I should back out. That her group was so much better, and she definitely dodged a bullet.

I'm such a tight ball of anxiety when I get to her apartment that I walk up to the wrong apartment and nearly knock.

When I trudge through the right door, Liz pats the spot next to her. I set the food on the counter and head over. Guess I'm ready to hear it.

As soon as my ass hits the cushion, she's on top of me,

lips on mine.

A laugh spills from my throat, interrupting her enthusiasm. "Are you trying to soften the blow?"

She sits back, her bony butt resting on my thighs. Her hands squeeze my shoulders twice. I squeeze her hips.

"Landon… I love you."

Uh oh. "I told you it was shi—"

She pinches my lips together, lifting a brow to make sure I shut up. "I love you. I love that you wrote such beautiful things. I love that it's very familiar." Her eyes sparkle, knowingly. "It's cute and fun and romantic. You have the rom com tone down."

"But?" I manage to push out around her fingers.

"It's a lot like us. A big chunk of it."

I nod. I know this. She's been my inspiration.

"And that, I think, is the problem."

My brows pinch together, and she drops her hand, pecking me on the cheek.

"Landon, you're way too close to it."

"I would think that's a good thing." Directors and screenplay writers always add a little of themselves into each project. That's why I love movies—or one of the many reasons. The relatability. Making it personal.

She traces the dinosaur skeleton on my Jurassic Park t-shirt. "I'm going to reiterate this, because I want you to hear it."

"Okay…"

"You are talented. Smart. And this movie you think is

shit isn't. Honestly, I would give it two thumbs up and hand you the grant money if I was in charge."

"You're a damn liar."

She gasps. "I am not, mister. And let me finish."

I pretend to zip my lips, but we both know that won't hold me.

"I'm saying that *I* would do that, because this was *our* story. I'm one-hundred percent biased."

I should be flattered and grateful she feels that way, but my head falls back, and I growl at the ceiling. I ask for help, which is the hardest thing for me, and I get this.

"Stop sulking and *let me finish*," she scolds, pulling me by the bill of my cap to look her in the eye. "I want you to think of your favorite movie."

"I don't have one."

"Now who's lying?"

I rephrase. "It'd be too hard to narrow it down."

"Okay, well try. Do the top ten, if that helps. Note the directors. See how many of them worked alone. Pay attention to what about that specific movie makes it one of your favorites."

I cock an eyebrow. "This will help my film?"

"Yes." Her confidence is contagious, and I've never shied away from studying. "What's missing is mass appeal. Take a step back and let someone else step up." She squeezes my shoulders. Twice. "You don't have to do this yourself. In fact, you *shouldn't*. To pull off a successful film, it takes a team." She reaches for my pocket, wriggling and tickling and finally getting my phone free. She scrolls for a minute, then turns it around. Jace's contact info stares back at me.

"Liz…"

"Landon." She shakes the phone. "Utilize your team."

SEVENTEEN

The clink of spoons against coffee cups fills the café near campus. It's mostly quiet—a few buzzes conversations. My knee bounces under the table, my laptop screen open to the notes Audrey sent over when I finally got the balls to give her access to the script.

The bell on the door dings, and I tear my eyes away from the red. Speak of the devil.

Audrey's gaze floats around the café until they land on me, then she smiles and heads over. I pull the chair out for her, and she slumps on it.

"Josh will be here in a bit. His class doesn't get out for another twenty."

"Jace, too." I adjust my hat, tilting it so I can see the screen better. Audrey takes off her jacket, and I feel her eyes on me.

"I was just looking over your notes."

She clears her throat. "Thoughts?"

Damn, am I that scary? I must be, because she's holding her breath. I need to chill the hell out if I'm going to be a good director.

The corner of my mouth lifts. "It's good stuff. I can't believe I didn't think to add a pool scene."

Her shoulders relax. "Definitely some opportunity for some chemistry building."

"And humor." I laughed out loud when I read the dialogue she suggested… plus the accidental flatulence. "Real quick… I know I think farts are funny, because I am a manchild. But will that fly with the female audience?"

"Farts are funny to a certain group of people, and that group is awesome." She grabs the table menu. "If it doesn't test well, we can scrap it."

"As long as you're okay farting on camera." I chuckle, adding the scene in the official script.

"I get to fart *at* Jace. I'm completely okay with that."

We work more of her comedy and chemistry suggestions into the script, enhancing what's already there. I feel slightly better when she raves about the declaration scene and tells me I better not touch it because it's perfection. The script is mostly ready when Jace and Josh arrive.

"We're scrapping the elevator," I tell them as they sit.

Josh lets out a gust of relief. "Good. My building manager was getting pissed, and I was dreading finding another location."

"Well… we need to find a hotel willing to let us film at the indoor pool. The campus one is way too large."

Jace puts in his order and then turns to me. "Actually, there's a rec center with a pool that might work."

Josh nods. "I was thinking that, too. I can check with both of them. See what's available."

"We'd need night shoots," I say, my knee starting to bounce again. I had this all on my to-do list—scout the location and book the shoot—and it's stressing me out by delegating.

Yet…

Josh did get that elevator stuff, and it worked perfectly with the lighting and set up. Jace recommended the section of the hotel lobby we shot so it wouldn't interrupt their day-to-day and we could shoot longer. Audrey obviously knows how to write.

I should've handed over some reins months ago.

I pull out my notebook and make four columns, marking each of our names at the top. "All right. We have a week and a half to get this thing shot and edited. You all ready to work your asses off?"

Jace puts a hand to his heart, gaping at me in mock shock. "You mean… we can actually participate?"

I shove him, even though he's dead accurate. "Yes." I turn to Josh and Audrey. "I'm sorry for having such a controlling bug up my ass."

They share a look, then Josh lifts a shoulder. "If we were really that bothered, we would've done something about it before now." He nods to the notebook. "Put me on location duty. I'll get those set up."

I write it down, and Jace and Audrey start taking on more. Jace begs to let him do some improv takes, and after a few minutes of giving him hell about it, I relent. He's funny, and I trust he'll give us some great material.

A couple of hours go by, and with all our assignments divvied out, we part ways. But not for long. Josh calls not twenty minutes later saying he's got the pool for the night for three hours. Liz isn't even bothered when I tell her I can't hang out because I have shooting to do.

The pride in her voice just makes it all the more motivating to work on this project. And damn it, I'm ready to win that grant *with* my group.

***

The lights in the auditorium slowly turn on, the sound of applause filling the room. Professor Driver steps out from left stage, clapping for Liz's group. "Great work, Team Horror. I think we all could use a little levity after that, so"—he checks his clipboard—"Team Romantic Comedy, you're up."

Liz squeezes my hand twice, and I lean over and kiss her on the cheek. Her group did fantastic, and Lizzie was stunning in front of the camera. She said she's not an actress by any means, and granted, it wasn't perfect and needed work. I would've shot a different angle, too. Her right side has this amazing freckle, and they always had her hair down. Don't they know how great Liz's neck is? Show that off.

I squeeze her wrist once and stand, the auditorium seat flipping up when I leave it. Jace hands off the thumb drive to me as I pass, and Audrey and Josh give encouraging looks. The color in my face must be absolutely gone if they're worried about me.

Professor Driver takes it, his smile almost like pity. He doubts we pulled it off; I can see that, and I don't blame him. We had a week and half to do the work we should've done all semester. Jace and I edited together, which was a whole new experience. I felt like I was teaching him, but he had some great insights, and it felt good to share what I've learned over the years. Instead of being self-deprecating the entire time, I was pretty damn confident in the finished product.

Professor Driver gets the movie set up, and the lights dim as I head to my spot next to Liz. The bunch of papers in my back pocket has me off center, but I don't take them out just yet.

She tucks in close, looping her arm through mine and resting her head on my shoulder. I'm a pile of nerves, wriggling and fidgeting as the movie appears on screen.

"Hey," she whispers, her breath tickling my neck. "Remember when I fell in the boob house?"

My nerves escape me with a laugh I quickly cover. I lean into Liz, bopping my forehead with hers. "You want to bring that up now?"

"Just trying to help you out, you nervous nelly." She tries to wink, but she's never been too good at it, half her face scrunching just to get one eye closed.

I kiss her lightly on the lips. "Thank you."

She'll probably never know I'm thanking her for more than just the distraction.

It feels like I've seen the film eighty times, but it's completely new when it's in front of an audience. Every laugh we get is a victory, every audible *aww* is another—especially when one comes from Liz. The fart gets everyone, and Audrey swivels to meet my eyes, and I silently clap in her direction. She bows, chuckles, and turns back around.

The final scene is my favorite, and it's bittersweet to see it end. Jace and Audrey slam dunk the kiss, and Josh panned wide, getting the hotel sign and fading out. N'Sync plays the credits, and Lizzie squeezes my side tight.

"Ah, you went cultured," she teases. I know I was supposed to take a step back from the personal stuff, but I had to keep something in there for her.

The lights turn up, and the applause muffles in my ears.

It's loud. Louder than I thought it'd be.

Though, that could be Liz, who is hooting and hollering and kissing my cheek.

Professor Driver walks out, stares directly at me, and claps. He mouths a single word, and I hope I interpret it right.

Wow.

I grin. Fill my entire soul with this feeling—this incredible, knock-it-out-of-the-park success. Then I pass it on to the people who deserve it.

I nod to Jace, Audrey, and Josh, directing the professor's attention to them. He claps louder for my group as a whole.

And I turn my attention to Liz. This response wouldn't have happened without her. This entire project, pulling my head out of my ass, learning I'm not meant to go through things alone…

I love her so damn much.

The applause dies down. Professor Driver moves on to the next film group. I'm up in the clouds somewhere. Even without the grant, I feel like I've won.

I set my hand on Liz's knee. Squeeze it. Twice. Then reach for the folded papers in my pocket.

The lights dim again as I bring them into my lap. Liz's gaze drifts, and when I catch her looking at the papers, I hand them to her. Tuck them into her palm. Kiss her knuckles.

"What's this?" she whispers.

"For you." I tap a kiss to her lips. "You asked me to make a list."

Her brow bunches, and she unfolds the paper, the rustling soft with the underscore of the film on screen. Her green eyes light up when she sees the title on the first page.

"Ooh. Looks like we have some movie nights ahead of us." She knocks into my shoulder, then starts reading. She doesn't know it yet, but I've just handed her the most precious parts of my heart, and they are hers forever.

Once upon a time, there was a kid with a giant dream. He saw worlds bigger than his own, elaborate stories he wanted to tell, and no captive audience.

He made it his mission to captivate every person he could the moment he saw this movie.

He hung the poster. Finished his first screenplay. Shot his first film.

It set him on a path. NYU. Major in film. Take the course that awards a grant.

Meet the love of his life.

And if all that comes from that path is you, it is a thousand percent worth it.

Epilogue

One year later

"You're really doing this?" Jace hunches over a display case, his face reflected in the clean glass.

"I didn't save all this money to not do it." I move to another display. My hand finds the back of my head, and I scratch at the hair poking out from the gap in my hat.

"You sure you don't want Liz to pick it out?" Alec asks from my other side. "She might want a say."

I shake my head. "I know what she wants."

Jace snorts. "Famous last words."

I ignore him. People will say we're too young and it's too soon, but they don't get it. I know Tumbles inside and out. And she sure as hell knows me.

Alec stuffs his hands into his pockets, moseying over to a display of necklaces. I'm pretty sure he's got a girl in mind, but he's being awfully quiet about it. I figure he'll tell me when there is something to tell.

Jace pokes the glass, getting a stern look from the saleslady. "She like these things? The big fat square kind?"

I shake my head. Liz will want one that's tilted on its side. White gold. Maybe a few accents. But simple.

My phone buzzes, and I check it, then nudge Jace. "Hey, we got approved for another three months for the studio."

"Nice." He pulls his phone out. "I'll order more blood."

He meanders away to do his thing, and I text Audrey and Josh the good news. When we were awarded the grant, Jace told them about my zombie script. After reading it, they both jumped on the chance to be a part of it. Josh became the location scout, and Audrey wanted makeup design and a small part. Filming started last January, right after Liz and I moved in together. It's been the best five months of my life.

"Finding anything?" Alec asks, and I tuck my phone away.

"Not yet."

He gestures to where he was just looking. "They have some over there."

I follow him past the necklaces and earrings, all too extravagant for my wallet. I'm skeptical as he stops in front of a very shiny display.

"Check it out." He motions to a set of some on the right, his finger hovering over the glass. "Maybe the second from the bottom?"

Alec must know Liz well, too. It's a thin band of round diamonds with a square centerpiece. If only it was tilted so it was diamond shaped instead of square.

"Yeah, that's okay."

"You need better than okay."

I nod. Liz would probably be happy with anything. Giant diamond, small diamond, dental floss…

But I won't. This woman is going to be my wife, God-willing, and I want to get her a ring that shows just how much I know her.

We walk around a bit more, and I'm about to give up when I catch it.

It's not in a display case. It's sitting out with a group of others in front of a couple. I rush over to get a better look.

Thin band. Modern. White gold. Tilted diamond. Perfect.

"Excuse me," I ask, realizing too late I've interrupted them mid-conversation. "Uh… Are you going to take this ring?"

The couple looks at the one I'm pointing to, and the woman smiles. "It's all yours."

"Thank you." I take it in my hands. So small but beautiful. I'm afraid to break it.

"You interested in this one, sir?" a salesman asks from behind the counter.

"Yes. How much?"

"Well, this is a very modest diamond. If you want an engagement ring, maybe something a little more—"

"How much?"

He jolts a little. "Twelve-hundred."

I raise a brow. "That's it?" Damn, I was expecting that to be the down payment.

"Like I said, modest."

My wallet is out faster than I can manage, and I fumble for my credit card. "I'd like it. Thank you."

"Payment in full?"

"Yes."

He takes me to the register, and I'm bouncing on the balls of my feet. Alec and Jace find me, smirking at my anxious fidgeting.

"Jesus, it's just a ring," Jace teases, patting my shoulder. But he squeezes it. We both know this is more than just a ring. But I'm ready for it. I feel like I have been since I pulled that chair out from under Liz's ass.

The salesman comes back with a black velvet box and my credit card. I tuck my card away while Alec takes the box, cracking the lid open.

"Damn," he says, showing it to Jace. "Our boy is getting married."

***

Keep reading for more of Liz and Landon in The Pleasure Pact

Thank you for reading!

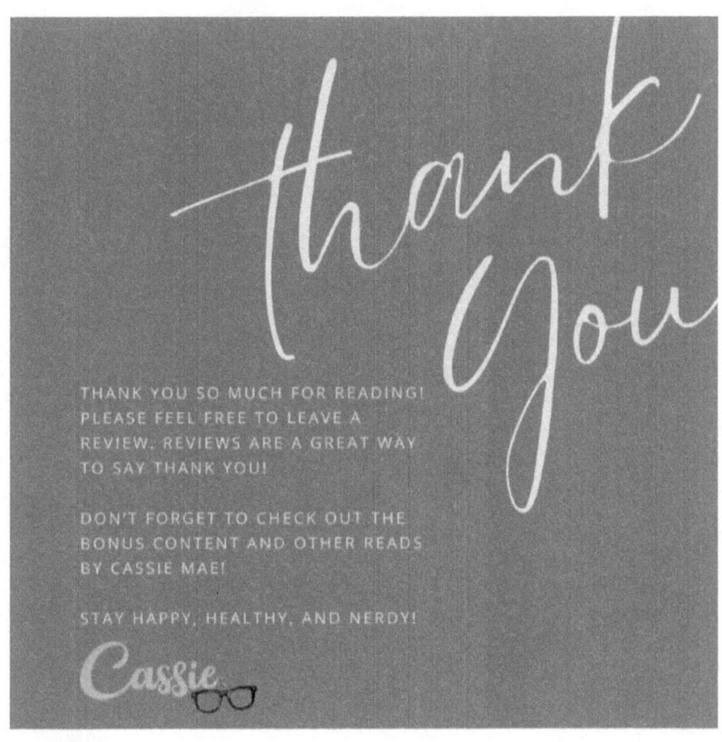

Sneak Peek of The Pleasure Pact
The continuation of Liz and Landon's story

ONE

Not pregnant.

Praise Jesus.

I chuck the negative test in the bathroom trash with a shimmy and a shake. Pregnant at twenty-two was not what I pictured when I did my aptitude test seven years ago. Those results said I'd be some sort of performance artist. I pictured me famous, in all the Broadway plays, living in my penthouse suite with my best friend, Theresa, and having weekend nookies with Chase Crawford. Kids were on the bucket list under: *hell yes…when I'm married.* Obviously, I was a dreamer at fifteen. Now that I'm more a realist, I've learned to be happy with whatever life has to offer me.

But I am happy that it decided not to offer me a baby *right now.*

I start the water on the shower because I feel like I peed all over myself when I attempted to aim on the stick. Aunt Flo is fourteen days late, and I've been avoiding Landon and his semen. Not that he's noticed.

If sex was a three course meal, Landon and I would be the peas and carrots. We're good together, but we're still the vegetables. Basically we do it when there's a commercial on, when there is no food in the fridge, or it's someone's birthday. It's okay… that's what happens when you move past the honeymoon stage.

We *used* to be strawberries and whipped cream. Luxurious dessert, grinding on each other on public dance floors, car sex, kitchen sex, against the wall sex, balcony sex—which was an epic fail, by the way—and the always disastrous shower sex. Disaster because our bathtub is made for one person only, and so lying down ended with a faucet to the butthole and standing up made for slippery recoveries. But we were strawberries and whipped cream, so we'd laugh it off, not let it break the mood, jump into bed, and keep at it.

I refuse to think we've become raisin bran—the sex you have only because you have needs to take care of—despite what Theresa says. She's permanently the palate cleanser between courses in her own sex life, and she's not budging any time soon. But she just hasn't found her Landon yet.

Anyway, back to Landon not noticing the lack of sex, it's because we're so busy all the time. He works all day at a call center then he goes and films all night. He's a director-in-training—got an award for his last movie and a grant to make the one he's working on now. So he comes home smelling like a sweaty sock—which he loves to leave on the floor in the living room. That's what peas and carrots do, though.

THE PLEASURE PACT

It's funny, for so long I wanted to know the story after the happy ending. What happens to the couple once they find each other, consummate their relationship, and get past their demons? Now that I'm in that story I get why no one talks about it. I'm in love, so it pretty much trumps all the other crap. At least, it has so far. Despite Landon's dirty laundry—literal—and his late nights—also literal—he makes me laugh. I've never had so much fun with another person. Even being vegetables, sex—when we have it—is *fun*. Probably why I wish we had it more.

Better check the effectiveness of my birth control first, though.

A hand whips back the shower curtain, and I scream like a banshee and chuck my washcloth at the attacker.

"Sweet mother," I say, holding my heart. "What the hell?"

Landon slowly peels the washcloth from the bill of his Nightmare Before Christmas hat. He's wearing his matching graphic tee, a red stain on the upper right sleeve. Probably from the pizza he had to gobble between his job and his shoot this afternoon.

"Liz," he says, holding the pregnancy test between two fingers. "What is this?"

"It's a negative pee test. Don't worry."

"Did you think you were *pregnant?*" He chokes on the word.

"Yes, but I'm not." I lean forward and kiss his shocked lips. "So *don't worry.*"

He lets out this large breath, chucking the test back in the trash. "Fine, but you must promise on your precious iPod that you will tell me next time you think you are."

I hold my hand to the square. "I vow to dispose of all my late period secrets." I drop my arm. "Now may I shower?"

"How long you going to be?"

"Normal."

"So till the hot water is out."

I put a finger to my nose, and he pulls his cap off. His shirt goes next.

"Joining me?" I ask, my lady nethers perking up. It's not even my birthday. What a sexy surprise.

"Yeah, I won't have time in the morning."

"Oh." Calm down girls, it's just one of those "saving water" things, and not due to the fact that I'm naked, he's naked, and we're going to be wet and slippery.

His cold hand splays across my stomach when he steps in, and I refuse to let my nethers get their hopes up again.

"You okay?" he asks, scruff tickling my neck.

"Yeah, why?"

"Paint me paranoid," he says, backing me into his chilled body. I move the water so he warms up. "But I think something's wrong. And I'm not letting you out of this shower till you tell me."

A twitch of a smile finds itself on my mouth. "I'm fine."

"Good thing you're naked." He taps my ass. "Your

pants wouldn't stand a chance."

I shake my head, biting back my laughter. "You're a tease."

"Why?"

He knows why. The last time we showered together he held me close like this, got me all revved up, then grabbed the soap, washed himself, and left for work. It's not his fault. I did the same thing the time before that. Again, comes back to being the veggies of the sex meal.

"Okay. The guessing game," he says when I don't answer. "I'll play, but you know I don't like it." He gently rocks me. "Your vampire show didn't record?"

I snort a laugh into the water. "I haven't checked. But it better have."

He swipes my hair off my neck, and I feel his smile against my skin. "Hmm… the Jets have no shot of making the playoffs. I feel your pain. I cried it all out last night. Now it's your turn."

I playfully elbow him in the stomach, but despite my abuse, Landon's arms tighten around me, thumb reassuringly rubbing my hipbone.

"No… I think I know what this is really about." He pulls at the skin by my bellybutton. I raise an eyebrow because there is *nothing* wrong. I'm just horny.

"Did you want a baby?" he asks, and my jaw drops.

"Huh?"

"It's okay if you did. I… I mean, I want to have kids with you someday."

Someday… yes. But not *today*. I grin at the scared-as-hell look on his face. That's the great thing about the longtime relationship. I know his looks. I know his smiles, his frowns, his laughs. I reach to him, and his hand slips through my wet blonde hair, hugs the back of my head, and pulls me into his shoulder. I lock my arms around his torso, ignore the sweet buzzing all over my stomach and heart and sides. His fingers massage my scalp as he rocks me.

"I like the idea of having a permanent piece of you," I admit into his wet skin.

"You already have a permanent piece of me." One of his hands slides down the length of my back. "Hell, you have the whole thing."

"You know what I mean."

"Okay… if you really want… I'll impregnate you. Open up." He pushes at my thighs, and I smack his shoulders.

"Pretty sure I want us to be married first. And I don't know… older." Like years ahead of us. We can barely afford to feed ourselves.

"You… you said married."

"I did."

I push back on his chest, and he scratches his dark hair. "Just letting you know I'm not freaking out about it."

"This is not freaking out about it?" I say, circling my finger at his face. It could be the steam from the shower making it smoke red, but it sure doesn't seem that way.

"I let it slide like it was nothing."

"You did not."

He growls, playfully nipping at my neck. "Well, I'm not freaking out," he muffles against my skin, creating goose bumps up and down my spine. "Because, you know, we're in the spot."

"Huh?"

"You know, the spot."

"In the shower?" I laugh when his red face darkens a shade.

"No, I mean… I love you. And it's not like I'm going to break up with you. And I'm pretty sure you want to be stuck with me."

"You think we're stuck? That's 'the spot?'"

"No. Shit, it's coming out wrong."

"I don't even know what you're trying to say." I laugh, bending down to adjust the heat on the water.

"I'm saying there's no reason for me to freak out because I want to marry you. I think, you know, we should get married."

My hand stops dead on the tap, and I crick my neck to catch his expression. He's gone from red wine to white in the blink of an eye, water dripping from his dark hair down his forehead, and he frantically wipes it away. Then he reaches for me, pulls me up against him, hiding his face.

"Um… what did you just say?" I croak, my heart suddenly beating out of my skull. A tidal wave rushes through my stomach, and my nails dig into his shoulders to make sure I'm not dreaming or something.

He slowly backs away from my neck, eyes wide as grapefruits. "I didn't mean… oh shit… it wasn't supposed to happen like this."

He falls forward, pushing me against the cold tile and hitting his forehead on the wall near my cheek.

"What wasn't supposed to happen?" I ask through a small laugh. Seconds ago he was boasting about not freaking out, and now he's gone bat crazy.

"I had it all planned," he grumbles into the tile. The echoes bounce off my shoulder. "I even bought a suit. Outside patio dinner, clear night for stars… I was going to pull out all the romantic stops, and it just falls out when we're in the shower."

"Landon, are you being serious? I can never tell."

"Because I'm never serious?"

"Pretty much, yeah."

He lifts his head, eyes meeting mine, and a nervous twitch pulls at the corner of his mouth. "Will you marry me?"

My heart's still thumping through my brain.

"The test was negative, Landon," I try to joke, but it comes out wobbly. "You don't have to—"

"I know." His palms cradle my face, drops of water falling from his eyelashes. "Will you marry me?"

His misty lips make contact with my nose. I'm still trying to process if he's serious or not.

"Really? This isn't because of that pregnancy test is it?"

"I was planning on asking a few weeks ago. Cross my

heart, the ring's been in this apartment for at least a month."

My eyes flick back and forth between his, searching, searching, searching for a lie, a joke, a tease, *something*. But it's all honesty and nerves and love. So much love I find myself slipping on the wall, losing strength in my knees.

"You *are* serious."

"I love you, Liz. Marry me? Please?"

I feel a smile tug on my mouth. The water's getting too cold to stay underneath, but my body temperature rises, my skin boiling under his touch. I grip his forearms, holding myself steady while he continues to cup my cheeks.

I love every bit of this man, every piece of his heart and soul and mind and body. So even though I wasn't expecting it this way, even though I was just internally moaning about not getting any spontaneous loving, I practically shout my answer at him.

"Yes."

"Yes?" He pulls back, hitting the stream of water square in the face. I laugh and bat it away from him. "Yes… you said yes?"

"Yes, I said yes."

A large relieved breath leaves his mouth before he presses it with mine. Landon's arms circle my torso, pull me up against his now hot and slick body, and every ounce of disappointment I was feeling evaporates into the shower steam.

"I thought I royally botched that." He laughs, and a wave of minty breath travels from his mouth to mine.

"You did," I tease before closing the gap between our lips again. "But I love you."

He tickles just under my arm, enough for me to jerk and slip in the tub. But his arms stay strong around my waist, holding me steady as his tongue glides across mine. Happy and excited whimpers somersault in my throat, and I know Landon loves when I make those noises so I exaggerate them a bit for his benefit.

His scruff grazes the hollow by my shoulder as he grips my right breast and slides down my body. More of those noises run wild over my lips, now one hundred percent legitimate, echoing around the shower walls. Landon's hands are all over me, slipping over the cooling water cascading over our bodies. His mouth keeps going down, down, down with aggressive kisses and nibbles, and my knees shake so bad I'm not sure how I'm standing.

Hell. Yes. Spontaneous nookie! I let my mind forget that it's a given since we just got engaged. I'm going to ride the hell out of him in the shower just like we used to. And after we slip, we'll keep on going in the bedroom.

I grip the top of his head and yank him up, wanting to kiss his mouth, his cheeks, his eyelids, his chin, his neck, his shoulders… but I grab too hard, and he yelps an "Ouch!"

"Oops," I say, kissing my fingertips and pressing them to his hair.

He rubs his head, water trickling down his upturned lips. "Didn't know you wanted it rough." His hand tangles in the wet strands sticking to my upper back, and he tugs enough to expose my neck. His lips tease and tickle just under my jaw, and I feel him smile right before his teeth dig in, and he sucks… *hard.*

"Stop!" I laugh, smacking his shoulders, propelling water in my eyes. "No hickey, no hickey! I have work tomorrow. Landon, I mean it!"

He suctions to me as I giggle and squirm underneath his strong hands. I manage to slide my hand down, lock tight around his arousal, and squeeze.

"Drop it," I threaten, slightly tugging. Landon laughs against my neck.

"You know that'll only encourage me," he says, thrusting into my hand. I quickly let go and spin around, pretending to get away, but I'm secretly raving about his arms catching me before I get too far.

"Oh, back entry!" he shouts when my butt smashes against him. I shush him in case the neighbors we share a wall with are in their bathroom. His voice lowers. "It's about time you let me do this. And to think, all I needed to do was propose."

He playfully jabs my left ass cheek, and I smack at his hands on my hips.

"You come near that hole, and I will flex my ass muscles so hard Little Landon will need six weeks to recover."

I shoot a wicked grin over my shoulder, and he gasps at me.

"*Little?*" He thrusts against my butt cheek again. "You

should call him Lord Landon."

"Because he rules your brain?"

"He rules the Land of Liz." Landon spins me around before I can even roll my eyes at him, but it's so slick in the tub we almost topple to the floor. I grip onto his shoulders while he holds the walls, and after we catch our breaths from the avoided catastrophe, Landon reaches around me to turn the water off.

"Bedroom?" I offer, and Lady Nethers jumps for joy when he nods, taking my hand and helping me out of the tub. As soon as both our feet hit the solid bath mat he pulls me onto his waist, not bothering with a towel.

"I just washed the sheets!" I shout as he throws my wet, naked body on the bed. He gives me a wide smile before sliding on top of me, and he's so slick he slips right inside. My eyes pop open from the unexpected entry.

"Oops," he says this time, but I don't think he's really that sorry about it. I start laughing and tighten my legs around his waist. Never mind about the sheets. We're not having peas and carrots sex right now. We're having *engagement* sex. And I like seeing all the water drip from the tips of his dark hair, onto my cheeks and nose and past my lips to my tongue. His playful grey eyes gradually dilate as he moves.

Laughter turns to deep sighs as Landon wipes my face free of all the water. He presses a soft kiss between my eyebrows.

"You're going to be my wife," he whispers, like a

prayer, a wish, a dream he never thought would come to life. My heart thumps between our bodies, thumps against his, answering his beats with mine.

"Mrs. Wangford." I bite my smile back, but it's no use, Landon pauses above me, his whole face lighting up.

"Hell yeah! Now you can't make fun of it."

"I'll say it in a seductive voice when I get my driver's license." I drop my voice an octave. "*Wangford.*"

"That's so sexy," he teases, biting my earlobe. I involuntarily giggle, goose bumps shooting up and down my entire body. That's totally my spot, and he knows it, so he runs his hands across my puckered skin while he nibbles.

"Okay... you have to stop laughing," he says.

"Can't be helped." I kiss his shoulder when he bumps it against my lips. "I *really* like it."

"I know." He bites again, causing more laughter and goose bumps. "But when you laugh, it does things. Down there."

"I know it doesn't hurt," I say, then flex my kegel muscles. He groans.

"No, it's just... we haven't done this in eleven days."

"You're counting?" When was the last time we counted?

He ignores me, resting an elbow on the pillow and using the heel of his hand to hold his head up. "On most occasions I purposely make you laugh because of how it feels." His lip twitches upward. "It's like a hug."

I stifle a snort, and he growls to the ceiling.

"Stop laughing!"

"I can't help it."

"You keep laughing, and I'm gonna shoot off before I can do my move."

"I've felt your move," I tease. "You need a new one."

His jaw drops, and his stroking fingers turn to tickle monsters up and down, down and up my ribs until he grips my sides and pulls me on his lap. My knees sink into the duvet next to his hips, and I run my nails through his damp hair. The stars in his grey irises seem to light the entire bedroom, echoing the moon dancing across the bed sheets.

I can't believe I get a whole lifetime of this.

"Me neither," he says, and a much smaller laugh tumbles out of my mouth. I had no idea my thoughts escaped me.

Landon's lips meet mine softly, then harder, then all over. My laughter, my mind, and body drift away into just one of the many beautiful moments I get to experience with this man. He feels so good, and the last time we had sex like this feels like a lifetime ago.

I'm just getting into my rhythm when I halt mid-hump with a gasp.

"What, what, what?" Landon says underneath me, sweat and shower water covering his skin.

"We need a condom."

He looks at me like I just spouted Greek. "Huh?"

"A condom, Landon. I stopped taking my pill a week ago."

"Why'd you do that?"

"I didn't want to hurt the baby… if there was one."

"Oh." He closes his eyes and nods. "Okay. Condom. Do we even have one?"

"Maybe…?" I'm being optimistic. I think I tossed them out during my last sex drawer clean up.

He slowly lifts me off him, and we both groan when we leave each other. I roll off the mattress, probably not looking so sexy with my naked squat and crawl to the naughty drawer in my nightstand.

"I could just pull out," Landon suggests as I dig around the lubricant, the sex tarot cards we've used maybe once, and the blindfolds we use much more than that, but not lately. There's not a single condom or any other form of birth control in here—unless you count the picture of my parents that must've slipped through the cracks from the drawer above it.

"I don't know. I think I'd rather be safe than sorry."

"But… we don't have a condom."

"Maybe Theresa does." Actually, I'm almost positive she does. I put the picture of my parents back in the right drawer and get to my feet. "I'll be right back."

"Your nipple is poking out," he says, pointing at my left boob as I shrug into my fuzzy purple robe.

"Thanks. Keep it up, will ya?" I point back at "Lord Landon" and speed walk out of the room, out my front door, down the hall, and rap on Theresa's door.

And just my luck, she doesn't answer. I slump back,

lady parts laden with disappointment.

"No?" Landon asks, still hard and ready on the bed.

"She's not home."

"I'll pull out," he says, grabbing the tie on my robe and ripping it open.

"Let me get a towel." I push him off before we get so into it I won't care until we have to clean it. Then I'll really care.

After placing the towel on the bed, Landon kisses me, probably knowing I've dried up and I'm losing whatever mojo I had ten minutes ago.

But we just got engaged, so no way in hell am I *not* having sex tonight.

ALSO BY CASSIE MAE

Love in New York Series
Master of the Meet Cute
The Pleasure Pact
Roadside Romance
The Date Dilemma

Give Me a Love Trope Series
Man in Uniform
Enemies to Lovers
Brother's Best Friend
Fake Relationship
Friends to Lovers

Nerdy Thirties Series
Flirty Thirty
Missed Kiss
Maybe Baby
Make Lemonade

Troublemakers Series
I Knew You Were Trouble
Double Trouble
Asking for Trouble

Join my ARC team for these books!

ACKNOWLEDGEMENTS

Thank you, Theresa. This book was completely your idea, and so I have you to blame for my endless nights writing it.

Thank you, Peach Rings, for being so yummy in my tummy. Sugar is my fuel.

Thank you, Mom, for teaching me that farts are always funny.

Thank you, Past Cassie, for keeping a series bible on this one.

Thank you, Tiffini, for every Wednesday. It is my favorite day of the week.

Thank you, Beta Girls, for always having my back.

Thank you, Willow Springs, for telling me to do better.

Thank you, Awesome Nerds. May the force always be with you.

Thank you, Jonathan, for listening to me list Landon's top ten movies even though you probably didn't care. I hope you enjoy Lebowski Con!

Thank you, Jenny, for being the bestest friend. I'm so lucky we were born into the same family.

Thank you, Rennie puppy, for asking to go outside every two minutes so my butt didn't go numb at my computer.

Thank you, children, for celebrating every single

chapter I finished with hugs and high-fives.

And of course, thank you, Joshy, for always squeezing my hand twice.

About the Author

Cassie Mae is the author of a dozen or so books. Some of which became popular for their quirky titles, characters, and stories. She likes writing about nerds, geeks, the awkward, the fluffy, the short, the shy, the loud, the fun.

Since publishing her bestselling debut, Reasons I Fell for the Funny Fat Friend, she's published several titles with Penguin Random House and founded CookieLynn Publishing Services. She is represented by Sharon Pelletier at Dystel, Goderich, and Burret LLC. She has a favorite of all her book babies, but no, she won't tell you what it is. (Mainly because it changes depending on the day.)

Along with writing, Cassie likes to binge watch Parks and Recreation and enjoys every Harry Potter weekend. She likes kissing her hubby, but only if his facial hair is trimmed. She also likes cheesecake to a very obsessive degree.

www.ingramcontent.com/pod-product-compliance
Lightning Source LLC
Chambersburg PA
CBHW031127130726
47988CB00006B/2262